# The Dutch Uncle

## P. T. O'Connor Investigates

Ed Kelemen

**Disclaimer**
This novel is a work of fiction. All of the people, places, businesses,
and events portrayed in this novel are either based on the author's
imagination or are used fictitiously. Even though the names of real
locations may be used in certain parts of this book, none of the people,
places, businesses, or events referred to in any of those locales are
intended to represent any relationship with any real events. Any and all
occurrences in this book are completely unrelated to the actions of any
real persons, places, businesses, or events and any resemblance to actual
persons, living or dead, or real businesses or institutions or to any actual
events or locales is entirely coincidental.

Published in the United States of America by
Nemeleke Publishing
New Florence, PA
Dec 2012

# DEDICATION

This book is dedicated to my wife of these multiple decades which have rushed by. Thank you, Lynnie, for all your patience, support, and love. I couldn't have done it without you.

# Contents

# ACKNOWLEDGMENTS

This book would have been impossible without the assistance, patient input, and encouragement of the members of the Greensburg Writers Group. To single out individual members for their insight, assistance, editing, gentle critique, and steadfast attention to continuity would be a disservice to all the other members of the group. All I can do is express my gratitude for all their unselfish help.

## Cover Design

The cover was incomparably designed by Lois Kalata, a graphic artist without peer.

My undying gratitude is extended to her for her great effort.

# CHAPTER 1 - RATS

Dead body in the boss's car. Liability insurance canceled for lack of payment. A million dollar lawsuit against the firm. The DA making noises about having our investigator's license revoked because he thinks we've got something to do with the aforementioned body. Moreover, it's all on my shoulders.

What in the hell else can go wrong on this miserably sweltering July afternoon in Pittsburgh? I pushed one side of the huge double front door open, remembered that I'd left something on my desk and turned to reenter the office. Just then a shower of splintering wood lacerated the back of my head. A split second earlier or two inches to the left and I'd be dancing with the Reaper instead of diving for the floor and rolling clear.

Just how did I find myself in this predicament...?

\*

My name is Pedar Timothy O'Connor. The only time anyone has called me by my full name was when my mother or one of the nuns at Saint Regis wanted to call my attention to some transgression or another. Everyone else calls me PT.

Six years ago, fresh out of Carnegie Mellon University with a degree in biological sciences, I answered a want ad in the Pittsburgh Tribune Review.

It read: "WANTED: Individual to assist in laboratory setting. Experience with lab rats essential. Call between noon and 4PM- (412)555-7287"

Having spent a semester running dozens of laboratory-bred white rats through countless mazes for statistical data in two college courses, I called that number. A voice that rumbled like summer thunder inquired as to my background in dealing with laboratory animals.

A stomach that likewise rumbled like summer thunder caused me to elaborate somewhat concerning my qualifications and affection for these little white rodents.

The interview took place at the offices of W.E.B. Enterprises at 4859 Second Avenue in the city's Hazelwood Section. The address seemed a bit unusual for a research lab. This particular section of the city, once a bastion of Scots, Irish and Middle European steel workers had, over the last few decades become a declining urban area. It had become an inner city slum in all but name.

As the fates and my bank account demanded, I answered Mr. Barrett's summons and went to the establishment bearing his name. My apprehension increased when I found a three-story yellow brick building sandwiched between the Thorny Rose Inn and a boarded-up five and dime. The first floor was devoid of windows. A stainless steel framed oaken double door was located dead center at street level. The second level had an elongated frosted glass window located above the entrance. The third floor had two windows, one on either side of the building's front. The overall impression was of a screaming face.

I stepped over and through the flotsam and jetsam that clogs city sidewalks everywhere and approached the imposing door. A closer examination showed it to be pock marked and scarred from years of urban battles. A small brass plate to the right was engraved, "W.E.B. Ent." Directly below was a push button. I pushed the button, heard a faint buzz inside answered by another, louder buzz which unlocked the door. I went in. Immediately inside the entrance door which I later learned was finished on the inside with a bullet and blast resistant acrylic, was an antiseptically stark foyer leading to a reinforced bullet resistant glass door furnished with electronic surveillance and remote operation just as the outside door had been.

I guess I passed muster because the inside door likewise indicated its approval by making a sound akin to a wasp too close to an ear. I pushed the door open and entered a twenty by forty foot reception area reminiscent of an English gentleman's club. Or, at least what I was brought to believe how one appeared from watching every James Bond movie ever made. The air was redolent of oiled leather and polished exotic woods.

Strains of Chopin played on what sounded like a harpsichord filtered through unseen speakers. It was an elegant escape from the dust, detritus and cacophony of the city just outside.

Expensively upholstered armchairs equipped with reading lamps and side tables were randomly scattered among the sumptuous sofas and coffee tables. As I wended my way through it dawned on me that they had been purposely placed that way. That prevented anyone entering the office from having an unimpeded route to the receptionist's desk placed midway along the left hand wall.

It didn't look like a place to harbor lab rats.

As I approached her, she looked up and said, "How can I help you, sir?"

A mahogany goddess spoke these words. Her feline gold-flecked brown eyes and beautiful face framed with soft curly ebony hair combined with the sexiest, most lissome voice I have ever heard, before or since. A long toned body gave the impression of a cougar on the prowl.

She had the effect of nullifying the quietly expensive air conditioning system of the building.

"I have an appointment with Mr. Barrett," I rasped, wishing my throat wasn't so dry.

"You must be Mr. O'Connor. Follow me, I'll show you to his office." To say that she walks is to say that Tony Bennett merely sings.

It wasn't until much later that I even realized that Monets and antique seafaring oil paintings flanked by discreet illuminating sconces adorn the walls, completing the calming effect of quiet harmony.

"Will – Mr. O'Connor to see you."

For the second time that day I entered another universe. There must've been fifty little wicker bird cages perched on every available flat surface in the splendidly appointed office. Most of the cages held at least four little white rats. A few cages were empty, the inhabitants having eaten their way through the wicker. Those escapees were now scurrying about eating their way through whatever else presented itself. Seated dead center in this pandemonium behind a huge and hugely expensively hand carved desk was an enormous black man.

"I give up," he said. He rose and offered a huge hand, "Welcome to Noah's Ark, Mr. O'Connor. I'm Will Barrett. I sure hope you can do something about these critters."

I could. I did. That was six years ago and I've been working for and with this fantastic man ever since. The rats were the property of the mahogany goddess in the reception lounge, Mrs. Barrett. Pamula Barrett had also been studying statistical psychology, only at the University of Pittsburgh in the evenings. When her experiment was finished, she didn't know what to do with the rats she had acquired. She absolutely refused to leave them in the possession of the University's animal husbandry department, not wanting them to wind-up as food for various raptors and lizards. Likewise, she didn't want to burden any of the city's animal shelters with them, being well aware of the shelters' criteria for euthanasia.

Her term at the University had been over for some six-odd months. White rats being mathematical little fellows and girls, the original two dozen had doubled, redoubled and multiplied until she had well over two hundred.

At that point she decided that the top floor condominium she shared with her husband on Mt. Washington just wasn't large enough and moved them into the office. Once there, they did their level best to drive Will Barrett out of his mind.

In a way, it didn't make sense that Will Barrett, who could solve almost any conundrum brought before him, couldn't find a home for a couple hundred little white rats. Well, he could. He just couldn't find a place acceptable to Pamula. She had grown fond of the little beasties and didn't want them harmed in any way.

In less than a week's time I had disposed of the rats to suitable quarters approved by Pamula herself. Kiddies at a children's zoo in the city where they are still happily procreating, many generations later, can to this day enjoy their descendants. In order that she wouldn't fret concerning the treatment of these pink-nosed creatures, a modest annual deposit to the zoo's operating fund guarantees that none will wind up as part of any scientific endeavor.

That's how I came to be a private detective.

# CHAPTER 2- RINKY AND DINKY

A tornado tore through the reception area leaving a scattering of tables, chairs and magazine racks in its wake. Will scrambled to my side, a huge 44 Magnum Auto-Mag dwarfed in his massive right hand.

Concern and confusion were fighting for prominence in his expression and voice as he blurted, "PT. What th- You OK?"

After verifying that I wasn't discoloring the carpet with any body fluids, I replied in the affirmative, stayed clear of the door, and regained my feet.

"Uh, boss? I think that 'little job' for your uncle may be just a wee bit more complex than we have speculated."

At the edge of my vision I could see Pamula returning the Ruger Mini-14 Carbine to its clips under her desk.

The maroon flush ebbing from his normally walnut colored complexion, Will replied, "Yeah, I think I'll have to make a few calls."

*

It all started a few days ago when the phone on my desk chirped. Pushing the little button that activated the speaker for the intercom I said, "What can I do for you, Will?"

"PT, come on in, I've a little job for you."

When Will referred to something as a, "little job", it could mean anything from a shoplifting at the corner grocery to the search for the elusive ghost of Elvis Presley. One thing for sure: a, "little job", is one that we do both gratis and discreetly.

I entered his rat-free inner sanctum, settled myself into my favorite of the leather chairs that half ringed his desk, and raised my right eyebrow quizzically. CNN was on the TV to the right of his desk.

"What's up?"

He asked, "Do you have that insurance case all wound-up?"

I informed him that it was in its final stages. The insurance agent who'd been in collusion with a string of body shops was in jail and the insurance companies were in the process of recovering what they could through the civil court system.

He nodded assent, muted the TV, and sat back in his chair giving me his full attention.

His usual soft, friendly brown eyes glittered with intensity and his face showed he was upset with someone. I was thinking, not for the first time, how that huge, hand-carved monstrosity that he calls a desk would dwarf anyone else. For him, it was a perfect fit.

"PT, someone's trying to shake down an old friend of mine. We need to find out who's doing it, why they are doing it and then make them stop doing it. Then we are going to put them out of whatever business they are in." He emphasized this last sentence by smacking his huge right fist into his cupped left palm.

I looked beyond him to the painting of the Cutty Sark, a nineteenth century clipper ship that dominated the wall behind his desk. His fascination with things nautical extended way beyond a painting and a desk made of the actual cargo hatch doors from the Slaver that had brought his ancestors to this country. The room also included many artifacts, all nautical, mostly navigational in nature. A gimbals equipped compass sat next to an ancient, but still working astrolabe. Quadrants, sextants and an inclinometer from a WWII U. S. Navy Destroyer were displayed beside a ship's wheel from an old Falls River whaler. A ship's bell, mounted on a wall was surrounded by antique navigational charts. The centerpiece of his book collection was an unheard of First Edition of Bowditch's, An American Practical Navigator, the navigational bible for seafarers everywhere.

Will always outlined objectives from the start. He prided himself in the fact that W.E.B. Enterprises always meets its objectives.

I shifted, popped a stick of gum in my mouth to replace the previously ever-present cigarette and asked, "OK, who's doing what to whom? Do we know why?"

"PT, you've never met Clarence Darrow Reynolds. He's close to seventy years old and he's been a Dutch uncle to me since I was a skinny little brat going to grade school. More than once, when dad was laid-off at the mill, Uncle Clarence would take him on at the scrap yard, even when he didn't need another man he could barely afford to pay."

Will's fondness for the old family friend was evident in his softened voice and the relaxation of the tendons in his neck.

"Uncle Clarence just called me and said that a couple of guys came into his office in South Side a few days ago and offered to buy him out lock, stock and barrel."

Pamula's selection of music for today couldn't overcome the pumper and ladder truck sirens from Engine Company 13 a block away heading for a call, "Sounds like a good deal for a seventy-year old man to me. What's wrong with that?"

Will's voice went from the pleasant basso profundo rumble of a bass violin to the threatening growl of imminent summer thunderstorms.

"The offer was so low that Unk said he laughed them out of the building. The next day, two of his men came to work wearing bandages and one called from the hospital to say that he wasn't coming in."

The high wail of an ambulance lent itself to the melody of mayhem in the city streets outside our sanctum.

Will leaned forward and snatched-up a yellow number 2 pencil from the blotter on his desk. He fondled it with the gentleness he intended for the throat of whoever was interfering with the peace of someone he considered family.

He brushed the pieces of pencil off his desk into a waste basket made to look like a coil of mooring line and said, "All three said that they had been jumped from behind and never even got a glance at their attackers. The assailants' m.o. is to knock the victim silly with some sort of a sap and then to rough him up once he's on the ground."

He rose from his chair and manifested his irritation at the harassment of his Uncle by pacing the room.

"Damn – they don't waste any time, do they? They went straight from shake-down to strong arm," I observed the obvious, while half-listening for the patrol car siren that had been absent from the chorus so far.

"Four days later, when Unk went to the yard to open-up for the day, start the compressors and steam plant, he found his three yard dogs dead. They had been poisoned."

Will's blood pressure and anger marched in lock-step as his frustration became evident.

"Slow down boss. You're turning maroon," I interjected. "I wouldn't want Pamula to think I was the cause of it."

"Later, that same day, he got a telephone call. He was told that the offer was being lowered because the new owners would have to invest in new guard dogs."

Will began randomly selecting books from the shelves behind his desk, opening them, closing them without even looking at the page and returning them to their niche.

This got my goat and made it personal for me, too. I don't know why, but I kind of equate poisoning dogs with taking advantage of kids. Both cases are a violation of trusting innocence.

"You know, Boss, it takes a real punk to poison dogs, someone with no decency whatsoever."

Will nodded, agreeing with my perception of the blatant.

"Within the week, four more of his men had been beaten-up, his steam plant sabotaged, his office trashed, and the windows of his car spray-painted during the night while it was parked in his driveway."

Will stopped pacing, turned to face me and continued, "After each occurrence, he got a phone call informing him that the offering price for the scrap yard was being lowered."

There it was: the sound of the city's finest heading for an emergency. A part of my brain hoped that their involvement would be limited to report taking and that nobody was injured.

Another part of my brain was telling me that I was going to get neck strain from trying to follow Will on his agitated tour of his office.

The main part of my brain heard Will go on. "The last straw was this morning. When he opened his mail, one of the envelopes contained a picture of his two granddaughters leaving home in the morning for work. That's all that was in the envelope, just that picture. Later he got a call asking him which is worth more: a scrap yard or a granddaughter."

Now he had one hundred percent of my cranial capacity concentrating on his words. Even in this day of enlightenment when the sexes are considered equal in every way, I have a hard time sitting still at the mention of a damsel in distress. I don't think that it is chauvinistic in nature, rather that it is my chivalrous tendencies exhibiting themselves. I stared at the sofa-sized painting of the battle between the Monitor and the Merrimack on the wall of the office to my right and clamped my jaw on my reply.

Will said, "Unk called his daughter, Celeste, to make sure the girls were safe. He said that he made it a conversational call so Celeste wouldn't get upset. When he asked her how the girls were doing, she told him that they were doing quite well and both had serious boyfriends now."

He picked up an excellent and working replica of an early 1600s quadrant from the shelves below the painting and sighted through it, as if making a navigational observation. That was his way of telling me that the conversation had ended.

"Got the picture, PT?"

Indeed. I had the picture and got to work right away on the problem.

It seemed straightforward enough: all I had to do was find out who was trying to intimidate Uncle Clarence, make them stop and make them pay. When put that way, it didn't sound complicated. Not easy, just uncomplicated.

I started that evening. I drove over to the South Side of the city. Not the trendy, pseudo-bohemian artsy-fartsy area where mixed drinks cost an hour's wage for an honest working man. And not one of the many quaint middle and eastern European enclaves that were populated by those honest working men. My destination was farther upriver to that area dominated by decaying hulks of warehouses, rooming houses, auto repair garages, beer joints and the South Side Scrap Works. I parked my car at a spot where I could watch the entrance until closing. I hoped that my car wouldn't be too obvious. It was, after all, clean and free of rust and beer bumps. Promptly at six the iron bar gates disgorged the working crew and I followed a few of them to their favorite watering hole, Rocky's.

Even with me right behind them, by the time I'd parked the car and entered the old mill gate bar, they already had shots-and-beers lined-up on the Formica counter before them.

I picked a stool toward the rear corner of the barroom where I could observe the activity and, in less time than it takes to tell, had a draught of that golden elixir known as beer foaming over the rim of the mug and making a wet spot on the bar in front of me. It was put there by a short, fat and balding guy with a three-day growth on his face. Tendrils of smoke dribbled upward from non-filtered cigarette clamped in the corner of his mouth. He wiped the moisture from his hands on the greasy, sweaty undershirt he wore and took my money from the bar in front of me.

He returned with my change and, a half-inch of cigarette ash defying gravity, said, "How 'bout them Pirates?"

His back indicated that no answer was required.

Sure enough, within a few minutes they came in. Two guys from central casting for an old black and white B movie walked through the doorway. You know the type: archetypical hoods.

One was relatively short, greasy and muscular. His swagger showed he was the leader. The other was tall, pockmarked and scraggly with an elaborate comb over. He walked with the elaborate hunched scuttle of the omega member of the pack. They both wore loose ill fitting and incongruously warm jackets on this summer evening. I mentally tagged them, "Rinky", and, "Dinky". They were uncommonly interested in the three from Uncle's place. There was really nothing to worry about for the moment – these three big men were in much better shape than Rinky and

Dinky dreamed of being.

Eight and ten hours a day of tearing down junked cars: stripping them out, removing glass, burning insulation off copper and aluminum wiring, jockeying them into the huge hydraulic compactor, then placing the cube of scrap on a railroad flatcar tends to keep one physically fit. It's what those loose-fitting clothes the hoods were wearing might conceal that could equalize the equation.

I try to avoid imbibing when working, but there are some places that a drink in front of you is de rigueur in order to blend in. In some other places the ingestion of that drink is also required to help one be absorbed into the scenery, such as it is. This was one of those places. People didn't go to warehouse district bars for a lot of social interaction. They went there to clear eight or ten hours of grit, dirt, dust, and rust from their throats. The fact that I wasn't wearing stained canvas coveralls or a mechanic's uniform was bad enough in this crowded working man's joint. There was no way I'd be able to fade into the background with a Pepsi in front of me.

After little more than an hour of shooting the bull and arguing over sports and politics, the workers kicked back their final shot of whiskey, drained their schooners of beer and headed for home. Rinky and Dinky followed them. I followed Rinky and Dinky.

Right away I smelled trouble. Not because I had any special nose for it, but rather because of the beer I had just ingested. Whenever I have a couple, I get what I call beer muscles. I become Super Sleuth, Righter of Wrongs and Solver of Problems. I tug my non-existent fedora a notch lower over my eyes and develop a certain assured swagger in my step. Rinky and Dinky disappeared around the corner of the building. The three men from Unk's split into two groups outside the bar. Two headed for one car and one for another.

I followed them, and was just passing the front of the scrap yard when Rinky and Dinky sped out of an alley in front of me and joined the convoy. I was so intent on not losing them that I nearly hit some kid on a motor bike. I swerved at the last minute and only got an impression of long blonde hair flailing wildly from under a helmet as the rider sped away. That deflated my beer muscles and reminded me that I hadn't visited the men's room before heading for the car. I kept the taillights of the convoy in sight and drove prudently, knowing that there was no turn-off for the next three miles.

When three of the four cars, mine included, took the ramp down to Old Streets Run Road, I killed my lights so the hoods wouldn't know that they were part of a parade. I also backed-off a bit more to give those in front of me some leeway to do their thing.

For a change, my nose for trouble was correct. I rounded one of the bends on this old road that follows the course of the particularly snaky tree-lined stream for which it is named. Rinky and Dinky's car was pulled-off on a wide spot to the side of the road, headlights illuminating a section of the stream's bank. Barely visible through the crushed vegetation, I saw the rear end of Unk's employee's car sticking up at an impossible angle from the stream bed.

Now, I may not always be the brightest bulb in the circuit, but even I could see they were up to something undesirable. The black plastic billys they held gave me a hint. I turned on the headlights, skidded to a stop and honked the horn while yelling out the window, "What's the trouble? You guys want any help? I called the police on my cell phone. You guys want a wrecker down here? Anybody hurt?"

They momentarily stood rooted to the roadside, as immobile and wide-eyed for the moment in the beam of my headlights as a deer in a spot light.

This display of idiocy had its desired effect. As soon as I yelled, that as a concerned citizen happening on a car wreck, I had called the police, they decided that a more efficacious plan would be to flee the scene. They regained their sense of self-preservation at the mention of the word, "police." Rapidly. So rapidly that one of them, I think it was Rinky, left his nasty little billy behind.

I picked it up, hoping to reunite it with its owner on an appropriate part of his anatomy at an appropriate time of my choosing.

I got their license number as they were leaving. Much as I would've liked to follow them, I had to stay and see what I could do for the yardman.

He was sitting dazed in the front seat of his three year old Chevy. The water from the stream had seeped up to his shin bones, but not far enough to have equalized the pressure on the outside and inside of the car. I had to pull him through the driver's side window of his car.

When I got him to the stream bank, his story was pretty much what I'd figured it would be. I was as close to an eye witness as could be without being a passenger in his car, but I let him get it off his chest. He'd left the bar and headed home. When he turned onto Streets Run Road, the large car had overtaken him and forced him off the road and into the stream. The impact with the stream bed must've knocked him silly, since the next thing he knew I was pulling him out of the car.

"Honest to god, mister. I thought I got hit with a tri-axle, it shoved my car so far," he said with that conviction only a victim of a traumatic incident can have.

I settled him in the passenger seat of my car and dialed 9-1-1 on my cell phone. Then we waited without talking, listening to the gurgle of the stream, the hiss of his car as it cooled in that stream and the hum of the insects who were now no longer disturbed into silence. Within minutes the police, an ambulance and a wrecker were on the scene. The police filled out their report of a hit-and-run with the information I provided. Unk's yardman told the wrecker operator where to take the car.

Mr. Tyler Wilson finally became someone other than an anonymous yard worker to me when I pulled him from the wreckage. Since he had sustained a mild concussion, the ambulance took him to a hospital for observation.

*

The next morning, I contacted one of my few friends on the Pittsburgh Police Department, Detective Sergeant Xavier O'Reilly of the Major Crimes Investigation Unit. He was able to match the license number on the Buick with a name and an address. By some sheer stroke of luck, the plate was neither fictitious nor stolen. The plate came back to someone with the unlikely moniker of Armand Mosticello. His address was in the city's Lawrenceville Section, a stronghold of Irish, Polish and Italian ethnic pride. It historically has also been a stronghold of organized crime.

That was because when times were bad and the city fathers turned their backs on the poor immigrants in a number of the city neighborhoods, the mob bosses took care of them with jobs, Easter hams, Christmas turkeys, and donations to the numerous churches in the blighted areas. Even though those days are long gone, habit has held a few of the old time mob types to the neighborhoods where they still enjoy a modicum of respect.

There are still certain sections of Lawrenceville where English is a second language. This address was in one of those sections.

After clearing-up some paperwork and making my oral report to Will, it was almost noon. I went to Scotty's next door for some Pittsburgh health food, a kielbasi and fried onion sandwich, before heading for Lawrenceville.

On my way out of the office, Pamula handed me bundles of stamped envelopes and asked me to drop them at the Post Office. It was the month's billings to various clients, checks for the operatives pay and bills, each group held together with its own rubber band, "gum band", to anyone from the area. We were paying some of the bills on the second or third notice. It had been a bit of a dry spell and finances were low. This was all the more reason for not taking-on gratis jobs. I intended to wrap this up as quickly as possible and start on some paying propositions.

If times were bad, you would think Will would just sell-off some of his expensive artwork to make ends meet. The truth of the matter is that times weren't bad for Will. They were bad for W.E.B. Enterprises, Inc. Most of the office furnishings were the personal property of either Will or Pamula. As a corporation, W.E.B. Enterprises had to succeed or fail on its own merits.

As much as I admired the both of them, I work for W.E.B. not Pamula and Will. I have a vested interest in seeing the company succeed financially.

This thought was uppermost in my mind as the door closed behind me on Pamula's musical selection for the day, something instrumental and evocative of Cole Porter on one of his blue days.

Waiting at the corner of Flowers and Second Avenues for the light to turn green, my attention homed in on a perky, sexy little blonde girl at the bus stop. The same thought crossed my mind that must have crossed my father's mind before me: they didn't look like that when I was in high school.

# CHAPTER 3 – MOSQUITOES?

Being one of those people who just like to drive sometimes provides unexpected benefits. Knowing the city as well as a cab driver is one of them.

Normally I'd drive over to the Mosticello address the short way, via Squirrel Hill, Shadyside and Morningside. However because this city only has two seasons, winter and construction, the short way was a maze of work zones with the traffic at each one controlled by a genius with a, "Stop or Slow," sign. I took the long way through the old industrial corridor to the downtown area, then out again through the warehouse district.

This led me along Smallman Street and Penn Avenue through the city's Strip District, a man-made ditch of warehouses, light industry, wholesale outlets, and the area's produce exchange. It was getting on in the afternoon and the produce yards were deserted. The activity around there peaked at four in the morning. At mid afternoon most of the street activity was due to the burgeoning rush hour.

A few more blocks and I was in the wholesale to the public section of "the strip." This area resembled nothing so much as the bazaar at the Kasbah. A kaleidoscopic mixture of color, people, storefronts and wares assault the eyes while a matching mélange of tempting aromas tempt the appetite. Even with the air conditioner on and the windows up, I could smell the Kielbasi, fish, tempura and spiced lamb cooking. As these enterprises close during the daily mad rush to evacuate the city, others open.

A few entrepreneurial souls discovered that the warehouses, school buildings and churches abandoned during the exodus to the suburbs were ideally suited for transformation into nightclubs of various genres. As the sun goes down, the lights come up and clubs for every taste rub shoulders with the slumbering daylight storefronts.

Once darkness settles over the area these expensive watering holes swarm with frenetic young people spending feverishly to push back the encroachment of involuntary isolation. Then the odor of flop sweat gradually replaces the exotic aroma of ethnic cooking and spices as the evening progresses and the miasma of loneliness pervades the choreographed hilarity of the club scene.

After a couple dozen blocks of this, Penn Avenue veers off to the right, Butler Street to the left. The "Y" of the intersection is occupied by a memorial to those who lost their lives in two world wars to protect this way of life. I veered left onto Butler Street.

Ten blocks of three story brick front buildings occupied by mom and pop stores, shot and a beer joints and less than successful attorneys, doctors, and insurance agents lined the way to Lawrenceville. It got its name from an honored statesman of Pittsburgh known for his wheeling and dealing strong arm tactics. Pretentiousness is non-existent in this refreshing in-your-face blue collar pocket kingdom.

According to the street signs, nearly fifty blocks have been traversed since I was in Downtown. I made a right turn off Butler Street, traveled a couple of blocks and turned left onto an anonymous side street. Mosticello lived on a meticulously clean street of two-story brick row houses, the kind that various developers unsuccessfully try to duplicate in the suburbs and call town houses. Each stoop had a two by four patch of dirt in front. Every patch of dirt exploded with the colors of peonies, marigolds, dusty millers, coleus and petunias. Each stoop also had a tree, usually a stunted hawthorn growing from a one square foot patch next to the curb. The only differences between homes were the front doors and the color of the drapes in the windows. Home owners in this neighborhood expressed their individuality by choosing which upstairs window should hold the humming air conditioner.

The address I sought was in the next block. Negotiating the narrow neighborhood streets required both skill and luck. With cars parked on both sides, once I committed myself to a block, I had to continue to the end of that block before I could either turn-around or avoid oncoming traffic. For a change I had a bit of envy for those kids running around on their whiny little motorbikes equipped with chainsaw engines. They could park anywhere. It was my lucky day: no traffic. Lady Luck still sitting on my shoulder, I spotted my quarry. It was in front of 4753.

I now had two immediate problems: keep an eye on the Buick and find a parking place. Not that there was a dearth of parking places. The problem was that the owners of each home consider that space of curb in front of their house to be their own domain, a personal and private reserved parking spot. Placing a couple of lawn chairs or kitchen chairs in that spot effectively reserved it. In Pittsburgh neighborhoods, it is an unwritten law that nobody ever moves another person's chair to get into a parking place. People have actually committed murder and mayhem over incursions into another's parking spot and Pittsburgh juries have considered it to be a justified action.

Driving around the block a few times wasn't an option either, since strangers and their cars do not go unnoticed in this neighborhood for long. I definitely wanted neither Rinky nor Dinky to find me in this area. I wondered which one owned the car.

I finally found a parking spot on a side street not too far away and walked back in the mid afternoon heat. I decided that my best bet would be to become an instant survey-taker. I started at the house on the farthest end of the block. An elderly lady with her head wrapped in the elderly lady uniform of Pittsburgh, the babushka, answered my knock on the highly polished door.

Giving her my best smile, I said, "Good day, madam. My name is Geoff Winters and I represent National Speed-Survey Incorporated. I am not selling anything. I would just like to get your reaction to the impending move of the Penguins National Hockey League Team from the Civic Arena to another venue."

I was the recipient of a distrustful stare and a wrinkled brow. Spreading her hands, palm up in the universal sign of incomprehension, she said, "No speaka Inglish".

Oh great. However, all was not lost. I figured I could kill a few minutes trying to make her understand with sign language. It wasn't to be. As I was trying to invent a sign for survey-taker, the highly polished wooden door slammed in my face. Getting pretty much the same results with the same conversational prelude three times in a row started a germ of discouragement in me.

Did you ever notice how your neck will manufacture its own grit, if it is both hot and humid enough?

I got lucky at the fourth door. There I found a Pittsburgh dialect English-speaking lady who was greatly interested in sharing her opinion on any and all subjects. To say that she was well-rounded would be an understatement. Everything about her was round: her face, the huge curlers in her hair, the penciled arch of eyebrows that gave her a permanently surprised expression, and the shape of the lenses on her blue-framed glasses.

Speaking around a lit cigarette while chewing gum she said, "No I don't think the Penguins should move from the Mellon Arena to another venue. Is a venue like an arena?"

I assured her that it was as I wiped a bead of sweat that had accumulated on my left eyebrow.

"Well then, they just probably want the city to build them a nice new place like the Stillers and Pirats got."

The dry dusty smell of hot concrete was making my throat wish for something cold, wet and carbonated, but she was on a roll and kept going.

"But yinz know that Lemieux fellow is kinda cute and he does live here, ya know."

She followed this up with a slight of hand that transferred the cigarette from her lips to her right hand while lifting a steaming mug to those lips with her left hand. Operation complete, she reversed the exhibition and wound up with the cigarette and mug back in their original positions.

"Yinz getting this all down?"

That gritty spot was oozing with perspiration that intended to tickle its way around to my Adam's apple. A few zephyrs of air conditioned air that escaped around her not inconsiderable bulk teased my discomfort.

Any attempt at disengaging from the onslaught of this lady's opinion was for naught. It took her a full forty minutes to run out of steam. By the time she was finished I had a crick in my neck from staring up at her from my less than advantageous position on the second step down from the front door.

Next door to Mrs. Loquacious, her neighbor held me in thrall for another twenty minutes or so. My impromptu survey taught me that this neighborhood was pretty much split down the middle regarding the Penguins' impending move. I also found out that Mrs. Patanyi made the best peroghis. Mr. Castalanna was running around on his poor wife while that floozy Bambi (now what kind of a name for a respectful woman is that) Cheszleski cheated on her hard working husband. Poor Mrs. Mosticello, a widow now, had to make do with what Social Security gave her while that unemployed bum of a son, Armand, drove around in a new Buick. My big time gangster lives with his *mommy*?

By now I had finished the buildings on one side of the street and was one-third the way down the other side when the door at 4753 opened and disgorged Rinky.

A mustachioed matriarch was in the middle of dispensing her advice and was not going to tolerate interruption. "…then you take a little of the liquid detergent and rub it into the stain. It doesn't work so good if you just pour it on."

I uttered my agreement with her stain fighting expertise as I watched the door to 4753 open and eject Armand Mosticello, propelled along by a torrent of Italian invective that originated somewhere in the depth of his home. He ducked his head in defense, strode to the Buick, started it, and disappeared in the direction of Butler Street.

"...you do that and just about any stain you got will go away in the wash. You don't have to bother with none of those stain fighters they show on TV. Yep, just two things that'll take care of anything: good old A-1 Bleach and rubbing the detergent into the stain."

Once again I thanked her for her insight into all things relevant to whatever my original survey question was and successfully made good my escape.

A three block sprint that ended as a sweaty trudge back to the company car left me thinking about what a wonderful invention air-conditioning was and how great it would feel once the car cooled down from its current molten steel temperature.

I ran my finger around my collar to allow a little air to reach the skin while the inadequate refrigeration unit tried to cope with the blistering heat, then engaged the transmission and pulled out from the curb. I was rewarded with that unmistakable flump-flump sound synchronized with steering pulsations: a tire was flat.

Inspection revealed a small laceration on the sidewall of the right front tire. The same size cut that you get from stabbing the sidewall with a pen knife, or a paring knife.

I didn't think that I'd taken anyone's parking space. I must've done something else to upset someone.

Twenty minutes later I had replaced the right front tire with the spare, muttering choice expletives all the while. By then I no longer noticed my gritty neck. That was because I had become hot, sweaty and gritty from head to toe as a result of changing the tire. I had barked the knuckles of my left hand on the inside of the fender and scraped through one of the knees of my Dockers. On top of that I was upset with myself for losing Rinky.

Thankfully, the lady who lived across the street noticed my predicament and brought me a jelly jar glass full of iced tea.

She probably wouldn't have looked so bad had she not been dressed for the weather. She wasn't all that overweight, but she tried to cool herself by wearing bright yellow short pants of the kind that had once been called pedal pushers by my mother. I think they are now called capris. This, combined with the white tube top encasing her ponderous breasts, reminded me of a pink, uncooked sausage about to burst its casing.

Never the less, at the time I had just finished changing a tire, not conducting a beauty pageant. Godzilla in a bikini would've looked gorgeous at that instant, had it been carrying an iced tea.

"Mrs. Thomasina down the street called and told me all about the survey-taker who was so interested in the Penguins. And I guessed it must be you 'cause I never seen your car around here before, ya know what I mean?

"Then I seen ya changing the tire- bad luck getting a flat on a hot day like this, ya know what I mean?"

I was too parched to speak, so I just nodded my agreement with her assessment of my current straights.

"So I figured that yinz'd like a glass of iced tea, ya know what I mean?"

I was grateful for the glass of iced tea that more than made-up for any lack of elocution that this nice lady had.

She went on, "It's a good thing you got back to your car when you did. A few seconds earlier and that crazy Armand would've run over ya."

"Armand?" I queried.

"I don't know what his hurry is all the time- he's just going to go to that damn club of his up on Liberty Avenue and sit around doing nothing all day."

I had forgotten the truism of Pittsburgh neighborhood life: everyone knows everyone's business. Maybe Lady Luck was starting to shed some compassion my way after all.

I commented on the fact that, in all my travels along Liberty Avenue near West Penn Hospital I had never seen a sign for a club.

She twirled a bit of grayish-blonde hair in her right index finder and said, "Well, it's not like it's a real club, ya know. Old Lady Mosticello once told me that it's up on the second floor of some Italian Restaurant in Morningside."

I replied that there is no shortage of Italian restaurants in Morningside and she said it was the one next to the old movie theater.

"So, now ya got your tire fixed, are ya going to survey me?"

I had already done that and found the location not zoned for anything beyond casual conversation.

"I'd love to, but truth is, I've got to get moving. I still have to cover another street over in East Liberty. Thanks for the iced tea, it really hit the spot."

She accepted the glass from my hand, her fingers curling over mine, and tried to coo, "Maybe another time, ya know…"

On the way to Morningside I made a mental note to find out how much those transmitting battery-powered GPS units cost. One of those in the wheel well of Rinky's' car and Lady Luck wouldn't determine the success or failure of the surveillance of a moving vehicle.

Mrs. Iced Tea's description of Rinky's destination proved accurate and I located the restaurant in short order. It shoehorned itself between an old dowager of a movie theater and an equally ancient shoe repair emporium.

Only a neon sign that said, "ood", identified it. The first letter which was supposed to be an F and a G alternately blinking was missing.

I was lucky enough to get a parking spot where I had an unobstructed view of the huge plate glass windows fronting this favorite eatery of applicants, supplicants and grantors of largess while remaining somewhat inconspicuous. There was a time when reservations would be required for a good observation point in this part of town.

That was during the heyday of FBI, ATF, state and federal Attorneys General Investigations. While we are at it, let us not forget the ubiquitous Grand Jury investigations of organized crime that never had an effect on organized crime whatsoever. All that law enforcement attention had one effect, however. The traditional crime organizations have moved out of what people think of as traditional mob crime areas.

The Jamaicans and other black groups have taken over the drug business. The Russians and Asians have taken over the prostitution and strong-arm business. The original mobsters are pretty much limited to gambling, loan-sharking and various forms of business crime.

Therefore, the old time crooks have gone to college, now wear suits and ties, and concentrate on, "White collar crime." Good old fashioned American ingenuity proved that unlimited dollars in profit daily flow from these crimes, with minimal risk.

For instance, in stock fraud and investment scams, a single caper could bring in millions of dollars. If the deal got busted, there was enough money already made to pay off some executive type for his lousy three to five years in a Federal country club with a lot left over for profit. For daily operating expenses, there was always gambling. The only thing more profitable than these fields of endeavor was politics. When you see some of the laws passed, deals made and millionaires created, you see the hands of these old timers in it.

I didn't wait long. In less than ten minutes, I saw a surfer-type muscle man enter through a back door inside the restaurant and gesture for Armand to follow him. Armand disappeared through that door to join him. The place was like a magician's hat, bigger on the inside than on the outside.

A little later a local personality followed Mr. Mosticello through the same door. Danny Saint Martin is a feature on both local television and in the regional papers from time-to-time for his "Underworld connections." While he wasn't among the ruling elite of the, "Families," he had a pipeline to them. Incidentally, his name was originally Dante Santa Marianno. He'd legally changed it to Danny Saint Martin years ago. That was possibly the last legitimate thing he had done. He clapped Mosticello on the back by way of farewell.

Armand made his appearance on the sidewalk carrying a large overstuffed brown envelope. He returned to the Buick, started the engine and just sat there. A couple of minutes elapsed and Dinky came out of the restaurant, slid in next to Armand and drove off. With the onset of rush hour, I was having a more difficult time keeping them in sight. On the other hand, with a lot more cars on the road, they would have a harder time noticing the tail. That GPS unit was already justifying its cost without me even knowing that cost.

Their errands on behalf of Danny Saint Martin really kept them on the move. During the next four-and-one-half hours, I followed them all over South Western Pennsylvania. They called on various politicians, police officials and businessmen in seven or eight communities south of the city. While I didn't have names, I had addresses and kept notes. This would have been a perfect situation for one of those new digital cameras with a telephoto lens.

As the evening wore on and traffic thinned out, I started to worry about being made. They seemed blissfully unaware of my presence and continued on their appointed rounds.

Finally, at nearly ten o'clock, it appeared that they were going to call it a night. They drove a relatively straight route through the South Hills into the city. The route they chose took us through Hays, Glenwood and Hazelwood directly past the motel where a compadre of theirs ended his career in the trunk of a Caddy, Mr,. Tyler Wilson's accident of the previous evening and the offices of W.E.B. Enterprises. I gave a fleeting thought to breaking-off and reporting in at the office, but I decided to stay with them and see to whom they reported next.

The Buick headed toward Downtown with me cruising about a half-mile behind. As we went by the industrial park where J & L Steel Company once stretched for better than three miles, they accelerated past sixty to seventy and then seventy-five miles per hour. This wasn't unusual, since there was no turn-off around here and the city police usually had something a tad more important to do than run speed traps. I accelerated to match their speed.

As I was passing where old Gate 65 used to be at the rolling mill, a pair of headlights suddenly appeared in my rear view mirror less than a hundred yards back. This clown had to be going over ninety when he swung out to pass me on the left.

Figuring it was just some semi-drunk idiot hurrying home to mama with an assortment of alibis, I slowed and tried to give him plenty of room to get by. As it went by, I could see that it was a huge older model Lincoln with black-tinted windows. I could also see a long, dark blue steel tubular object extending from the open rear passenger window in the general direction of my head.

I guess it was the adrenaline. I was able to do three things at once. I wrenched the wheel to the right, dove for the floorboards on the right side of my car and muttered,

"Cell phone...cell phone", just as the driver's window of my car exploded in a shimmering cascade of glass.

I felt my car slam over the curb under the Birmingham Bridge at Brady Street, then carom aimlessly off various items of unquestionable solidity. When the car came to an abrupt stop against something immovable, I lost consciousness and dreamed of mosquitoes.

Mosquitoes?

# CHAPTER 4 – A SUNDAY DRIVE

An incredibly bright light stabbed through my closed eyelids. I regained a state of semi consciousness. My brain was arguing with my feelings. Brain said, "Let's wake up and see where we are." Feelings said, "Uh-uh. We don't want to know."

The combination of the smell of alcohol, iodine and disinfectant mixed with the unmistakable odor of pain, fear and uncertainty convinced me that this was no upscale residential establishment. The constancy of bustling people, squeaky wheels and the tinkling of glass against metal started me thinking in a certain direction.

It all became strictly academic when a disembodied but distinctly female voice said, "He's coming around now. Call in that police detective who's so anxious to see him."

I opened my eyes. The light source was a two-foot wide examination light in what seemed to be a cubicle in a hospital ER. A monitor to the left of my bed was making video game sounds while squiggly lines marched across it in a kind of spastic orderliness. I didn't know, or care, which hospital. Hell, I didn't even know what day it was.

I closed my eyes.

Soon I heard the slapping of leather on tile heading my way. I opened my eyes again. I should've kept them shut. I greeted one of the city's finest with what I had hoped would be enthusiasm, but instead sounded like a ruptured toad croaking, "Hi Brannigan, take up ambulance-chasing?"

The large florid gentleman who was there to investigate my "accident," informed me that not only did he not chase ambulances, but his name wasn't Brannigan.

"Shallenberger. Valentine Shallenberger. Detective second grade Valentine Shallenberger. You can call me Sir."

He said it with the same lack of inflection that a famous actor used to say, "Bond- James Bond."

With his beefy red countenance, icy blue eyes, and fire-engine red hair, I just thought his name should be Brannigan.

I filled him in concerning the drunken idiot who'd forced me off the road. Beyond that, I related nothing, because I had once again surrendered myself to the temporary possession of Morpheus, caretaker of dreams.

Somewhat dissatisfied, the detective left after a bout of prodding by the ER nurse, who told him his time was up. The next thing that impinged on my consciousness, or lack thereof, was a light tap on my shoulder accompanied by Will's concerned voice.

"PT, you OK?"

I opened my eyes and grunted. Then I returned to the realm of Morpheus to see how the dream involving me and a plethora of pulchritudinous young ladies evolved.

\*

Some two-and-a-half days later I departed University Hospital, the closest one to the scene of my "accident." Luckily, I hadn't lost my memory while in a state of suspended animation. A very cute and simultaneously insistent nurse making me feel helpless, took me to the patient pick up exit of the hospital in a wheel chair. As I rode home with Will in the black Impala, he filled me in on what had happened after I wrecked my car.

"About three in the morning, the phone rang. A voice said that if I ever wanted to see you again, I should look around the construction site on Second Avenue by the Birmingham Bridge."

I abhor riding in a car that someone else is driving, even if that someone else is as accomplished a driver as Will. I found myself wishing that he would pay attention to his driving and not to me.

"The caller also said that if we didn't back off on the scrap dealer investigation; the next place to look for you would be inside a two-by-two-by-two metal cube, just like the ones at the scrap yard."

Will was driving along Fifth Avenue in the direction of my apartment just a bit faster than I liked. However, I kept my opinion to myself and simply mumbled something about my dislike of cramped spaces and Will went on.

"I called Nick Moore and told him to meet me at the construction site."

To take my mind off the ride I studied the people walking along the sidewalk and scurrying out of our way at intersections.

Will said, "By the time I arrived, Nick had already called for an ambulance. He found you at the bottom of a concrete piling form."

The scurrying made me think of the rats I'd freed Will of. That, in turn, made me think of mazes. This of course logically brought me to the conclusion that we are all prisoners of mazes of our own construction. Concussions must affect my thought patterns in strange ways.

I returned my attention to Will who was still talking.

"Here's what we figure happened. You were forced off the road and into a pile of gravel. Then someone pulled you from the car, stripped you naked and pushed you into the form where cement was being poured the next day."

I said that I could see where that just might suffice to harden my resolve. Will graciously ignored my feeble attempt at levity, swerved to miss a PAT Bus and kept on as though there had been no interruption.

"You were out until sometime the next afternoon. During that time one of the buildings at Uncle's scrap yard burned to the ground and another of the yardmen was met that night and convinced to find employment elsewhere. Then Uncle got another phone call telling him to sell out within a week or the deal would be completed with his heirs."

I accepted Will's explanation. After all, he was there and I was in Elysian Fields when most of it happened. Beside, I didn't want to say anything contradictory that would distract him from his driving.

"Sounds about right to me. There are only a couple of things that don't add up," I replied.

"First, if I was naked in the bottom of a concrete piling, why didn't the police or someone mention it?"

Will replied that Nick had found most of my clothes scattered around my car, along with the contents of my wallet, sans currency. I started to relax, realizing that we were getting closer to my home.

"Second, I feel like someone did a rain dance on my body before throwing it into the concrete form. I owe someone for that."

Will advice was that we should all endeavor to pay our debts and that he considered this one personal. If I weren't so sore in so many places, I might have felt sympathy for those who engendered his ire. Plus, I longed to reunite that billy club with its owner.

"One more question, Will. What about the guy that tried to kill me with the shotgun?"

Damn! I should have kept my mouth shut. Thank God that Sunday afternoon traffic is relatively light. Will turned to look at me in astonishment, then returned his gaze to events happening along our vehicle's projected trajectory. Those events caused him to utter an expletive and apply the brakes with gusto, thus avoiding destroying the second company car that weekend. He was effusive in his apology, fearing that the strain I placed on the seat belts may have somehow exacerbated my injuries. I hastily assured him that I was in no more physical pain than when I entered his death trap of a car.

It was apparent that he didn't know about the man with a shotgun.

We finally arrived at what I call home: a small two bedroom house overlooking the city from one of the high southern hills.

I thanked Will for his concern and the ride home and turned the air conditioner down to something approximating meat locker conditions and then, paradoxically enjoyed a scalding hot shower.

A stiff drink was called for under the circumstances, but the doctor had advised against the ingestion of anything alcoholic until the effects of the concussion had completely worn off.

Before climbing into a nice soft bed I checked my answering machine for messages.

There were just the usual messages that I tend to get from family and friends, including a frantic one from Beth who was in Chicago for the weekend. I returned Beth's call and assuaged her fears before crashing into bed.

One message stood out from the rest. A voice muffled in such a way that it wasn't possible to even determine the sex of the caller said, "You are a dead man, you bastard." I copied the number from my Caller ID and went to bed.

# CHAPTER 5 – DEAD DINKY

Monday morning dawned bright and cheerful. I was neither.

I shaved and showered, then dressed in clean, comfortable clothes that wouldn't rub on my newly acquired scrapes. I watched the local news: nothing about me. Drank a bit of coffee. Paced around. Called a cab and went in to the office. I figured I could have aches and pains at the office as well as at home. Plus, there would be people there to hear me bitch and complain.

On the ride in I wondered at the fact that I can ride comfortably with cabbies, bus drivers, and Beth but no one else.

At least on the ride over the weather changed to match my mood. It was getting overcast and threatening. By the time I was dropped of by the cabbie at the International Headquarters of W.E.B. Enterprises, the sky was spitting those one ounce drops that fall right before the big storm.

As soon as I arrived at the office, my first order of business was to show Pamula my war wounds and get my fair share of sympathy and commiseration. I hobbled over to her desk and she said, "PT, you're late. Will's been waiting over an hour for you." With that, she handed me a sheaf of envelopes, papers and magazines that represented the outside world's acknowledgment of my existence. So much for sympathy.

"Tell him I'll be there in a minute."

As I headed for my office, I could hear happy strains of today's musical selection coming through the hidden office speakers. It had something to do with being King of the Road.

I popped into my office, started brewing a pot of my special mix and booted up the computer. Most of my mail and incoming faxes could be trashed simply by scanning the return addresses. It is astounding the amount of mail we PIs get from people wanting to sell us spy vs. spy equipment, mostly illegal. Like I would actually buy any of that stuff via mail or over the Internet with a check. Besides, most PIs I know would be much more interested in a ergonomic car seat.

By the time I'd sorted the mail into a stack to read and a bag of confetti in the trash, the coffee was ready.

I filled a mug, stopped by Pamula's desk to scoop up a doughnut, and went in to see Will. I sat at my usual seat on the comfy leather chair that was second from the right in the seven chair semicircle facing his desk. It was the one that afforded me the best view of the painting behind his desk.

"How are you feeling today, PT?"

Unlike most other people, Will was actually concerned with my well-being and wasn't merely opening a conversation with a hypothetical question. I assured him that I had mostly healed from my miscellaneous and sundry scrapes, abrasions and contusions. I still had a nagging headache from the concussion, but Will didn't need to know that.

"Good. I guess all those hours you spend at the gym and on the water aren't wasted."

That's Will's way of showing me he approved of my twice-weekly stints at the gym and my passion for white water kayaking because they helped me avoid missing work due to injuries received on the job. I made a mental note to check with him later to see if I could charge the company for some of the expenses incurred while pursuing my passions.

"Yeah, well the doctors told me that, had I not been in such excellent physical condition, I might have sustained some permanent injuries from my experience. I just wish that I would have had the chance to bruise my knuckles on a certain head instead of my car fender," I said and took advantage of his reply to lick powdered sugar from my lips and sip at my coffee.

"PT, this has gotten a bit more involved than I'm comfortable with. I don't want to expose you to this kind of danger. After all, this is my problem, not yours." He was making marks on a paper with a colored pencil.

I let Will know that he was family and that any problem of his was a problem of mine.

"Besides," rubbing a particularly troublesome spot in the vicinity of my left temple, I said, "Now it's personal."

"OK, OK," there was both relief and gratitude in his voice, "Don't go off half cocked. Unk wants to meet the young man who has been going to all this trouble on his behalf. He is hosting a barbecue at his daughter's place Saturday. You're welcome to bring a friend."

I said that I'd be delighted to attend and Will said that he and Pamula would be there as well.

"Oh, and another thing. I didn't want to bother you with it while you were home and hurting."

"Shoot."

"We got trouble." He continued to scribble on the paper. I wondered if he was ticking off items on a list.

I gave a somewhat perfunctory wave of my hand and, talking around a piece of doughnut, said, "We always got trouble. That's the nature of our business, seeing as what we offer can be seen as troubleshooting."

"Cut it out, PT. I mean *we* got trouble. And we just might need the services of another kind of troubleshooter: attorneys."

Uh-oh. Will was serious in a way that I have seldom seen him. He even seemed worried.

"What's up?"

"At some point after the "accident," the towing company delivered your car to G & G Auto Repair, the place where we have the company cars serviced. The insurance adjuster showed up promptly this morning at 7:00AM and declared the car a total loss. He then began to catalog the damage to the vehicle. When he opened the trunk, a cadaver with a dented forehead was grinning at him."

Oh Great, just great. I could see where this was heading.

Will continued to ruin my morning, "When the police arrived, they photographed the body from every conceivable angle before touching it. A wallet found in the trunk with the body belonged to one Joshua McClymonds. The photo on the driver's license, allowing for the caved-in forehead identified the corpse as that same person."

"Uh Will? Any idea on the cause of death?"

He rolled his eyes and spoke slowly as though to a ten year old, "The caved-in head, along with a tire iron covered in tissue and specks of bone seem to point to what the authorities are fond of calling blunt force trauma.

"Additionally, McClymonds, if that was who the victim actually was, was wearing an empty shoulder holster."

The police forensic unit towed my car to the crime lab for additional processing. Motor vehicle accidents usually don't include a blown-in window and shotgun pellets in the driver's side headrest. Neither was any paint from another vehicle found on my car. All these things made it unlikely that my car wound-up totaled because someone sideswiped it.

Detective Second Grade Shallenberger called Will and mentioned his disappointment with me for my lapse of memory concerning these aspects of the accident. Will had given him my home address and told him that I was probably there, still having been a bit shaken from the accident. Detective Shallenberger and his partner were going to be even more disappointed with me when I wasn't home.

Whatever Will was putting down on the piece of paper must not have met with his satisfaction because he suddenly crumpled it and tossed it into the waste paper can next to his desk.

You know, I hate it when the local minions of the law are upset with me. It tends to make Will uncomfortable. Will then tends to make me uncomfortable.

Hands out, palms up in supplication. "What do you want me to do about it, now? I was just protecting an investigation. Besides, you didn't say anything about me being beat-up, hog tied and naked in a concrete form, did you?"

He set down the mug which had nearly reached his lips and said, "No, but the tow-truck driver has put me at the scene as well. Shallenberger was making noises about conspiracy, accessory before and after the fact, and violation of the private investigators code of ethics."

"Huh, code of what?"

"It looks as though the only way to clear this up is to find the killer."

It looked that way to me, too.

I moped my way back to my office, sat down behind my desk and stared longingly at my Wall of Infamy, a collection of broken paddles, bent karabiners, and pieces of frayed rescue line. I had earned all of them whilst enduring the displeasure of the River Gods on various stretches of whitewater.

A light came on in the dim recesses of my skull. That's what I needed to stretch the muscles, clear the cobwebs and chase the punies away: a river trip.

The weather had looked as though it was going to dump big time on us today. That meant that, just maybe, some of the smaller streams might fill up with water by the day's end.

"The Mile," on Slippery Rock Creek would do nicely. A relatively short, but challenging stretch of whitewater with lots of play areas and some pools between rapids for resting that was only forty-five minutes away. A couple of phone calls and I could set up a trip for late this afternoon. I brought up my address book on my computer.

The intercom interrupted my train of thought. Pamula told me that I had visitors from the police department.

I sighed, cleared the screen, and said, "Send 'em in." I felt more like committing a homicide than discussing one.

It wasn't Shallenberger and company. It was the, "Fraud Squad," as they liked to call themselves. They liked the way it rhymed. Damn, some guys are easy to please.

Detective Murray Williams entered the office, made a bee line for the coffee pot, helped himself and wearily lowered his rumpled body into a chair. He sipped at his coffee, placed the cup on the table and raised those sad brown eyes that have seen everything and can no longer be surprised.

His voice, as sad as his eyes, he intoned, "'lo PT."

I waved acknowledgment in his direction and said, "A grand and glorious good morning to you as well, Murray."

Meanwhile, the fidgety half of the team, Kenny Kennedy, scurried about. He got himself a cold can of soda from the 'fridge, found a brownie in there as well, placed a brown paper bag on my desk, shook my hand, said, "Thanks for handing us the chop-shop case," and finally settled into another of my chairs, at least for the short term. He was a Jack Russell Terrier to Murray's Blood Hound.

I opened the bag. It contained a fifth of Irish whiskey and a gift certificate for a case of Guinness Stout, two of my favorite things for cleansing myself of common sense.

I was embarrassed.

"Hey guys, you didn't have to do something like this. But hey, really...thanks."

I was speechless and just let my voice trail off.

"It wasn't my idea," said the verbose Murray.

"Yes it was", said Kenny rapid fire. "He said that it was the least we coulda done considering how you laid the whole case out in our lap all wrapped up with a bow and all. He said that it wouldn't do no good to tell your boss how we appreciated your help and all because you are already the fair haired boy around here. He said that you'd probably appreciate the whiskey and beer more than a pat on the back."

Murray contrived to look uncomfortable as though this revelation of his less jaded side was a betrayal.

He said, "OK, O'Connor, we just need your taped version of what happened for the DA."

"Yeah," said Kenny, getting up from his chair and moving around, "Murray figured that, by taping your statement, maybe you won't have to testify in court."

I shoved the fifth of whiskey toward the edge of my desk closest to them and raised my eyebrows inquiringly.

The both shook their heads side to side, Murray muttering something about the sun still being below the yardarm.

I knew what was on their minds. By taping my statement for the DA, there was a good chance that I wouldn't be called as a witness in the case, thereby giving them 100% of the credit for solving it.

So I told them, "The way I look at it guys, it's just one more day that I won't have to wear a suit and tie."

One they saw which was I was leaning, they relaxed, although it is hard to describe Murray being more relaxed than he was. It was also unclear to any but a trained observer that the wired up Kenny had relaxed.

I gave them the statement that they wanted. It was a pretty straightforward case once I'd done a little digging.

So, feeling a bit stupid for talking to a tape recorder while two other people were in my office, I started. This is how it went-

Will had gotten a call from a loss prevention department of one of the insurance companies that have a contract with us. One of their agents seemed to be steering all of his clients to a trio of body shops. It smelled of kick-back and Will dropped it in my lap to clear it up.

Once I got into it, it went deeper than just a kick-back scheme where the insurance agent gets a percentage for steering customers to certain shops. In that case, the shops can justify it as a, "Finder's fee." Then the insurance agent is guilty of only breaking company rules and a code of ethics.

In this instance, the insurance agent was covering all bases in the supply and demand process. First, Joe Blow would notify the agent that he'd been in an accident needing body work. The agent would then inform the customer that he could probably work out something to cover his deductible with one of the three Dent-B-Gone body shops in the area.

The next step would be to call his Dent-B-Gone contact and tell him to expect Joe Blow to be coming in needing body work and trying to work a deal on the deductible. He would then check all the policies that he'd written looking for the same make and model that Joe Blow had. Once he had located one, he told his contact at Dent-B-Gone where to find it.

The Dent-B-Gone people would then steal it and use its parts to fix Joe Blow's car at below list and everybody was happy. Joe Blow got his car fixed and saved his deductible. Dent-B-Gone fixed Joe Blow's car without buying parts and pocketed the profit. Jack Blackburn, the agent for Consolidated Collision Insurers put a couple thousand in cash aside for a rainy day. John Doe, who'd gotten his car stolen, got a new car for the cost of the deductible. The only loser was a faceless conglomerate insurance company who had to lay out a couple hundred thousand dollars to keep Dent-B-Gone and Jack Blackburn in pocket jingle.

Another thing, the stupid asshole never even considered what was going to happen to his wife and two teen-aged daughters when he went to the slammer. Besides losing everything they thought was theirs; they are going to be painted with same brush as their loving husband and father.

Saying their farewells, the sad old bloodhound and his counterpart the hyperactive terrier made their way out of the office. I gathered up the debris that they'd left in the form of coffee cups and napkins, cleaned the crockery, and tossed the rubbish. I replaced everything that Kenny had touched, moved or rearranged and the place was back to its pre-visit state.

I went back to my plans for the visit to Slippery Rock Creek. As I was nursing my bruises and contemplating a refreshing mid summer run on the 'Slip, this middle-aged guy came walking in and announced himself to Pamula. She filled out one of our client information cards: name, address, occupation, etc.

He identified himself as one Wallace Locke, vice president of distribution, Universal Steel. He sported a Fox Chapel address.

Pamula brought Mr. Locke to see me. Luckily, the only outward evidence of my escapade with Rinky and Dinky was a scrape on the side of my jaw that could be a result of overzealous shaving and a little hitch in the way I walked. The scrape would be gone by the weekend. Hopefully, the hitch would be worked out on the river tonight.

During my six years with W.E.B., I have become a junior partner. I share income and, to a degree, decision-making for the firm. I also serve as a buffer between Will and the mundane. However, whenever Will and I reach an impasse, Will's opinion prevails.

My office is neither as large nor as luxurious as Will's. Nevertheless, it is a tastefully appointed place resembling nothing so much as a place of work an attorney would covet. A large walnut desk with the ubiquitous computer and telephone reigns over a semi-circle of comfy armchairs. A bookcase containing mostly river guides to the Eastern United States and law books pertaining to riparian rights dominates the left wall. The right wall has a credenza which is actually a wet bar and two doors: one to the bathroom and one to the outside. The wall directly opposite my desk contains my collection of broken kayak paddles and other flotsam from the rivers.

Wally Locke was a medium. I don't mean he had anything to do with the paranormal. Its just that he was medium height, medium build, medium aged with a few strands of medium brownish grey hair strategically brushed across a forehead that had gotten as high as he was going to allow it to get. He wore a medium grey business suit with a white shirt and a maroon tie. He was so colorless as to vanish when trekking the canyons of Downtown Pittsburgh during business hours. Here in the land of serapes, dashikis, jeans and work clothes, he stood out like a clown at a Mennonite prayer meeting.

I asked how we might serve him. I also offered him the libation of his choice. My wet bar has everything from skim milk to blue flame rum. He opted for a plain, unsweetened iced tea. I joined him with my own blend of freshly ground decaffeinated Colombian and caffeinated Brazilian coffees.

Once he was comfortably ensconced in an armchair with a side table, I repeated my original query. After some fidgeting and false starts, he opened up.

"Mr. O'Connor, I think my wife is cheating on me. I hope she isn't, but I think she is. I'd like to put my mind at ease. So I would like you to find out if she is or if she isn't. There will be no messy divorce involved so I won't need any pictures, videos, wiretaps or witnesses. I know that you are expensive, but you are also the best and I can afford it. When can you start?" He paused to take a sip of his tea.

Honest to God, that's how he talked. A straight monotone with neither modulation nor pauses. I added periods and commas so you could understand it. He issued it in a steady stream of words.

Now you may have heard of detective agencies that refuse to do domestic investigations. If you have, it was probably some TV or Hollywood agency that doesn't pay rent or other expenses. I personally have never heard of an agency refusing domestic investigations. That's because they are the bread and butter of detective agencies. If you pay the bill, we'll investigate absolutely anything, so long as it is legal. Or at least quasi-legal.

Only one other service provided by a private detective agency brings in more income: uniformed security guards and night watchmen.

I explained what services he could expect for his money, concluding with, "Our basic price is $500 a day, plus expenses for a simple daylight tail. Twenty-four hour coverage runs the bill up to $1,200 a day."

Mr. Locke stretched his bloodless lips across his teeth in a parody of a smile, "Plus expenses, of course."

I smiled back, "Of course."

He signed a contract for a two-week job, forking over a personal check for three thousand dollars as a retainer. I gave Pamula the paperwork and entertained Mr. Locke a while, getting all the particulars while she verified that his check would land in our account with a thud and not rebound with a bounce.

He expressed interest in my collection of broken kayak paddles. While I didn't give him the grand tour, I did point out the paddle that had its shaft broken while I was taking a particularly nasty line on Pillow Rock Rapids on the Gauley River in West Virginia. Next to the carcass of the paddle is a picture of the rapid where it met its demise. If you look closely you will see the front tip of a blue kayak barely breaking the surface in the whirlpool called, "The toilet bowl." More than one river vidiot thanked me later, saying that my spectacular crash and burn on that day sold extra copies of their videos.

By the way, vidiot is the term that whitewater videographers use to describe their chosen profession. They are a special breed of extreme whitewater paddlers who race ahead through some of the most horrendous whitewater in the country just to videotape the paying customers as they ride the rapids on guided trips. The vidiots paddle their way through in a nine or ten foot long kayak. The paying customers ride a ten person raft that is steered by the guide. Before I met Beth I called it a ten man raft.

Mr. Lock stared pensively at the collection of paddles as well as some of pictures of the incredible whitewater found within a few hours drive of Pittsburgh.

"I wish I could afford the time away from work to pursue such a bobby," he mused unconvincingly.

I forced myself away from my wall of infamy and returned to the matter at hand, saying, "Mr. Locke, exactly why do you think your wife may be cheating? Is there anywhere in particular that you would recommend we look?"

I finished my second mug of coffee that day while I listened to that familiar dreary tale of an older man who snared a trophy wife. Man married to his job as much, if not more than to his wife. Lots of money for her to play with and become bored. Lots of enticing outside activities to involve herself in. Plenty of unfettered men to entertain her who weren't married to their profession or anything else. Unexplained absences when he called home during the day. Unexplained mileage on her car.

What a lot of men fail to understand is that a trophy wife is like any other trophy. She must be earned, not bought, otherwise she will tarnish.

I could see it written in capital letters across his forehead: ant married to grasshopper. Older ant married to younger grasshopper at that. He works non stop toiling for times of need; she was enjoying the good times while they lasted.

*Laissez les bbon temps rouler, "Let the good times roll," as they say in The Big Easy on Fat Tuesday.*

It was so typical and elementary a job that I gave Will only the most perfunctory description of it and assigned it to one of our free lance operatives.

"This way we can save both time and money on this case. One of our outside men can handle this for $250 a day, plus expenses and we can just pocket the other $250. Easy money."

"Which outside man?" He wanted to know.

"Nick Moore," I replied.

He grunted his approval.

I returned to my office feeling rather satisfied with my business acumen, and mentally placed the Locke case into the profit column.

I once asked Will why he didn't spruce up the building's exterior. Or even just uproot the entire operation and move it to a more prestigious location in Shadyside or the suburbs. He told me that there were two reasons. First, he would never desert his old neighborhood. Second, he likes the reaction from unsuspecting would-be clients who wander into the place expecting to find some seedy, two-bit operation and instead come face-to-face with a $200,000 interior decorating job. At that point, some of them even turn tail and escape with their wallets intact. The ones who stay, don't. W.E.B. Enterprises doesn't work for peanuts.

This satisfying reverie died a quick and violent death due to some kind of commotion in the lounge. The red, "Get your butt out here NOW," light was flashing on my telephone console so I made quick for the front. Will and I nearly collided in our haste to get to Pamula's aid.

Two men loomed over her desk. One of them was loudly demanding the presence of both Will and I. It was the same large red-headed, Irish looking detective that I had met fleetingly at the hospital.

"Well, if it isn't Detective Second Grade Valentine Shallenberger, or should I just call you Sir?"

I didn't know, or didn't observe at our first meeting that he was also fashion-challenged, to be politically correct. I didn't realize that a man so large could get a coat to hang so loosely on that not-inconsiderable frame. A bit of tailoring might have cured his droopy-drawers problem as well. The mismatch of patterns, colors and styles between his coat, shirt, slacks, and tie made me think that he had been the victim of some cruel practical joke.

"Manny, the wise ass with the strawberry blonde hair is O'Connor," then, to me he said, "Are you trying to give me the slip?"

"Quite the contrary, good sir. I have been patiently awaiting your arrival here for quite some time. Obviously we are victims of cross communications. Please accept my apology," I said, watching his complexion blend with his hair.

I tend to get sarcastic in the face of bombastic self-importance. I can't help it.

Will was not in the least apologetic, sarcastically or otherwise. Apoplectic was more like it.

Adrenalin was coursing through his body performing all its assigned chores. It raised his blood pressure and increased his heart rate to insure adequate oxygenation to his major muscle groups. His pupils dilated to increase his field of vision and visual acuity. Blood sugar was elevated to provide readily available fuel to the major muscle groups. Blood flow was redistributed to his major skeletal muscles. In short his fight or flight response had kicked in. He was not going to flee.

"How dare you come to my place of business and harangue my operations manager, who just happens to also be my wife. I'm sure that a quick call to the Police Office of Professional Responsibility will rectify this matter."

The intensity of Will's emotions was evident in the way his body was involuntarily assuming a threatening position regarding the visitors. Forcibly clenching his fists at his side to prevent using them as weapons, he continued, "I don't remember that bullying young women going about their lawful business as part of your job description. That is, if you continue to even have a job after our lawyer gets involved."

I had to hand it to them. They didn't back down in the face of this onslaught by this huge black man whose musculature threatened to destroy his expensive custom-made dress shirt. Shallenberger acknowledged Will's presence by merely lifting an eyebrow and turning in his direction. His partner, Manny, used his unremarkable features as protective coloration, blending into the background like an interested spectator. His attire at least matched: grey coat, grey slacks, off-white shirt, and maroon tie.

The pair of cops complemented one another the same way as "Off," and, "On," on a light switch.

Now it was Pamula's turn. "Oh Will, PT, I was so afraid, I didn't know what to do." She fluttered her fingers aimlessly in the air as she said, "When these gentlemen showed me their badges over the closed-circuit TV, I never thought they would come in here yelling and threatening me. You'll see what I mean when you look at the surveillance tape." She even threw in a catch in her voice for good measure.

Shallenberger quickly backed up. I think it was the phrase, "Surveillance tape," that caught his attention. His partner merely contrived to look confused.

"Maybe we were a bit overzealous here, but after all, there is a murder involved."

That was about as close as Shallenberger was going to get to an apology.

"Certainly detectives, we understand how it can get. I tend to get a bit protective where my wife is involved. Now, what can we do for you?" Will was showing his magnanimous side now. His mercurial change in attitude caught our visitors off-guard.

They warily kept a protective distance between themselves and Will, fearing that this bi-polar monster might abruptly shift personalities without warning.

Will likes to keep a select few people off balance that way.

We all wound-up in Will's office a few minutes later seated in front of his desk while Pamula got coffee for our guests.

I swear Shallenberger flinched when Pamula, after placing a cup of coffee at his elbow, picked-up a leaded glass canister containing sugar cubes and inquired, "One lump…or two?"

She then gave him a saccharine smile and undulated from the office, with eight appreciative eyes following her.

When the last of her passed from view, we returned to the matter at hand. Shallenberger tasted his coffee, smacked his lips and said, "That's a good cup of joe. But, come on, O'Connor, level with us. What in the hell is going on?"

I answered his question with one of my own, "Why, what do you mean, detective?"

He was more passionate than called for when setting down his cup and some of the hot liquid slopped over while he said, "Don't get cute with us."

Then, as he mopped up his spill with the dainty little napkin that Pamula provided him as a coaster, he turned in Will's direction and wheedled, "Mr. Barrett, tell him not to get cute with us."

I was just starting to have fun and hoped that Will would give me free rein when the grey ghost of a man next to Shallenberger spoke up for the first time, "Listen, guys, look at it from our point of view."

He motioned in my direction and said, "One day O'Connor here is a whupp-ass victim in a hospital. A couple of days later a body with skinned knuckles is found in the trunk of O'Connor's car."

Then, turning toward Will, Todd continued, "And O'Connor won't say anything more that he was in an accident and don't remember nothing else."

I nodded. Shallenberger nodded, whether in agreement with me or with Todd, I wasn't sure, but he said, "What we've got here ain't no accident, it's a homicide."

Like an agreeable bobble-head doll, Todd mirrored his partner's head motion and said, "You two haven't been exactly forthcoming with us, have you?"

With a barely perceptible lowering of his left eye lid, Will gave me the go ahead to open up.

I took a swallow of my coffee, cleared my throat and tried to be as truthful as I could without compromising our client. I explained that I was tailing Armand in his role of bag-man as he carried payoffs to various and sundry people, including members of the law enforcement community. Forestalling Shallenberger's protestations on behalf of his brother officers, I said that it was a surmise on my part. I had no real proof.

I got up from my seat and sat on the edge of Will's desk to better face the police officers.

"At some part during the evening, Armand must've gotten wise to the fact that he had a tail. In this day of modern technology, it only took a quick call on his cell phone to set-up the ambush."

The ambush occurred in the most desolate section of Second Avenue. I told the detectives that I knew nothing about a shotgun blast: I assumed that the shattering of the window was part of the wreck. Anyhow, I remembered nothing after feeling the car go over. Then next thing I knew was waking in the hospital with Detective Shallenberger's comforting countenance filling my field of vision. His promise to bring the full force of the police department into the investigation of my, "Accident," was more than enough to once again instill in me a sense of personal safety. That feeling had been lacking since I went for a loop-de-loop at the hands of some maniac.

I finished my coffee, set the cup down and concluded by saying, "No, I know nothing about any body in the trunk."

Will picked it up from there, explaining his part in my rescue. He didn't mention finding me hog-tied and naked. He did say I was still unconsciousness when he arrived. He spread his hands wide in a gesture of openness and said, "You can check it out with the ambulance crew if you need verification. When we got there, PT was lying on the ground away from his car, as though he'd been thrown clear during the wreck."

Shallenberger replied, "Yeah. We're one ahead of you there. We already talked to the meat wagon boys and they pretty much corroborate what you've been saying."

Beyond that, Will stated that he didn't know much. He'd called for the ambulance and wrecker and made arrangements for what was left of the car to be towed to the repair shop. After neither the car nor I were any longer at the scene, Will had gone home.

"Now I ask you, Detective Shallenberger, how could either PT or I tamper with evidence in a homicide case when neither of us even knew that a homicide had taken place? As far as I was concerned, the nearest thing to a homicide at that location was PT's being run off the road."

Now Todd had an inquiring mind, an asset for a detective. He set aside the notebook he'd been scribbling in and answered Will's question with another, "OK, if everything is on the up-and-up, then how do you explain your presence at the scene?"

Mustering all the innocence that his face was capable of, Will replied, "I got a phone call telling me that one of my men had been in a wreck and telling me where. It was in the middle of the night. Until I got there, I thought the phone call came from you guys. Now, I don't know."

Indicating by a shrug and a head tilt that he didn't believe a word he'd heard, Shallenberger opened a manila envelope, extracted file folder and selected a photo from the file. He slid it across the desk to Will and asked, "Do you recognize this man?"

Will replied in the negative and handed it to me.

I took it from Will and looked at it. Now I knew him by a name other than Dinky. The label on the photograph, besides having the case and property numbers of the incident, also said that the subject was one Joshua McClymonds. I commented, "The last time I'd seen him, he was alive and riding shotgun next to Armand Mosticello in the front seat of a Buick."

That was an unfortunate choice of words. Shallenberger either didn't notice or chose to ignore and he continued. He said that McClymonds was a small-time hood, a wannabe gangster, always hanging on the fringes of organized crime, but never quite making it into the club. He'd had a string of arrests, mainly for minor stuff like booking bets and switching registrations on stolen cars. He had two traits: he was never around when things went poorly for his associates and he had a reputation for welshing on bets.

I had the feeling that these detectives had hidden motives for bringing out this dog and pony show for us. Something about Shallenberger and Todd made me feel hinky. I just couldn't put my finger on it.

Anyhow, he gave the usual lecture about not leaving the area without notifying him, and gave us one of his cards. His partner grunted in support and they both left, Shallenberger perching a cream colored straw hat on his head. Then, Shallenberger stopped, snapped his fingers in the air as though he had forgotten something, turned around and returned, stopping in front of me.

He reached inside his coat and withdrew a folded paper, handing it to me, saying, "Oh by the way, here's a warrant for the clothing that you wore when admitted to the hospital. Do you want to give it to me, or do you want us to stop by your digs and search for it?"

Without giving me a chance to reply, he turned on his heel and rejoined his partner.

As they left by way of the front entrance, I found my voice and called out, "Sorry about your color blindness."

One of them replied, but I must've heard him wrong because it was impossible to comply with his request.

After they departed, the three of us convened at Pamula's desk. She stayed seated at her desk while the two of us were sitting on opposite corners of that desk munching the morning's pastries.

"You know," Pamula observed, wiping a bit of powdered sugar from the corner of her mouth, "I think that PT was set-up from the beginning."

She had our full attention now.

"PT, remember how you were able to see everything at the restaurant through the window? And you were a half block away?"

"That's right."

She swiveled her head side to side to include us both in her comment, "OK, now is it possible that Saint Martin and his go-fers were just trying to give you a run-around for a few hours while something else was coming to a boil?"

I rolled my eyes and tried to focus on one the Monets nearest her, trying to remember if that particular one was a copy or if it was one of the other ones. I felt what was coming.

She continued, "After all, they didn't do anything all evening to shake a tail or even to check for one. Right?"

Will cut in, "I think you're on to something, hon. PT, what do you think."

Think? Hell, my head hurt while the obviousness of the ploy sunk in. What better way to get a PI off your butt than to give him something else to investigate?

As I headed back to my office, Will said to my back, "You better make arrangements for the gumshoes to pick up your dirty laundry if you don't want them rooting around your house."

I called back, "Yeah and what do you think the chances are that they'll return it cleaned and folded?"

# CHAPTER 6 – THE THORNY ROSE

I zig-zagged through the maze of furniture back to my office, all the way mourning the river trip that wasn't going to happen that day. I felt that the best thing to do was to cleanse my consciousness of the case and let my sub-conscious take over. Further, the best way to empty my mind of everything else was to try to avoid giving Uncle Sugar and all his destitute relatives eighty cents of every dollar we earn. The state legislature's latest pay grab brought on this attack of parsimony. That's an endeavor that requires full and undivided concentration. A couple of tax-exempt municipals looked attractive, but the minimum purchase was in 10,000 share lots. It seems to me that, if local governments want citizens to invest in them, then the minimum purchase lots should be small enough for the average guy to buy some. Plus these bonds have sticky rules about premature redemption.

I was getting nowhere. Which would be OK if nowhere is where I wanted to go. Everything I looked at had some drawback: hefty penalties for early withdrawal, deferred payments and long-term asset holding. I just don't trust any investment that can't be liquidated whenever I get the urge. Sometimes bills that won't wait propel that urge. Then I get upset when some mealy-mouthed broker tells *me* that I can't have *my* money.

I could now add headache to the rest of my aggravating ailments. I resolved to turn the whole investment mess over to someone who knew more about such things, and was trustworthy, competent and honest. I hope I have better luck than Diogenes and Lot.

I started wrapping-up for the evening with the intention of having a quick one next door at the Thorny Rose Inn.

The phone emitted that aggravating nasal beep that is supposed to be a ring. It was my private line. I picked it up and announced, "O'Connor."

"P-T, it's Exie. We need to talk. Where can we meet?"

I could tell from both his choice of words and his tone of voice that he didn't trust the privacy of my telephone connection.

Exie and I go all the way back to high school. We were students together at Central Catholic. At the time, everyone thought he was going to be a priest and I was going to be a teacher. Instead, he became a city cop, working his way up to the rank of sergeant in the Detective Division. I... well, I yam what I yam, as Popeye used to say.

"How about the Scotsman's place?" I suggested.

"OK, see you there in a half hour."

The Thorny Rose Inn is not quite a misnomer. It definitely can be a thorny place on occasion. It just as definitely is not an inn. It isn't even called the Thorny Rose Inn, except on the liquor license and the faded neon sign over the door. When the "T" on the sign burned out, Scotty, in spite of the majority opinion of his customers, never turned the sign on again.

In the late seventies, the steel industry went belly-up. The reasons for the collapse have been the subject of books, speculation and political campaigns.

Books, speculation and political campaigns have never put food on the table. Hazelwood, like so many other mill towns in the Steel Valley endured a rapid decline that took nearly a quarter century to reverse. Due to this decomposition of one of the city's most vibrant areas, crime became rampant.

For a few years Second Avenue was a no-man's land, entered only by predators and the strong. The occasional foolhardy innocent who entered the fray quickly became prey for the raptors that nested in the darkness.

Scotty redid the tavern's original glass storefront in modern American Fortress architecture. It consists of a solid steel door flanked by two glass block windows. The steel door is equipped with a peephole so that Scotty DeGuerre can observe prospective customers before admitting them after the sun sinks into the west. This innovation was installed after the Thorny Rose, known to habitués as, "Scotty's", had been held-up three times in one month.

Eventually a class of people newly graduated from colleges, trade schools, and the military discovered the bargain in the area's housing. These people weren't going to stand for the kind of activity that the area supported and they started the climb back to respectability.

The abandoned J & L Steel Mill was razed and turned into an industrial park giving a home to new, upscale cyber businesses. This brought an influx of computer engineers, programmers and the like to the area. Like the steel workers before them, they wanted to live close to their work. Housing and housing prices in Hazelwood became desirable again.

All this had no effect on Scotty's philosophy of business. Even though the stocky, grizzled ex-steelworker was on the forefront of the battle to reclaim his home, neighborhood and business, he used the peephole in the locked front door after dark and kept the loaded 12 Gauge under the bar.

The door pushed open away from my hand with a ponderous slowness and I entered a throwback to the heyday of the shot-and-a-beer mill gate bars. It was a place where hard working and hard drinking men could gather on their way to and from work to either prepare for or recover from eight hours of hot, sweaty, bone crushing, back breaking, filthy work. It made no pretense of being other than what it was: a bar. There's no piano, no dancing girls, no entertainment other than that generated by the habitués. In the old days, before my time, this kind of establishment was called a beer garden.

A twenty foot wide room greeted me. The right side of the tavern displayed a long hardwood bar with a dozen or so red Naugahyde and chrome bar stools lined up at attention. The left side had eight Formica-topped tables, each with four cane-backed chairs. A black-and-white tile floor and some yellowing pictures of local sports heroes completed the décor.

I greeted a couple of the regulars who were nursing draughts at the bar, said hello to Pat Fitzgerald, nodded through the back bar mirror at Harry Sweeney and patted old Tom Long on the back as I passed by on my way to Scotty's position near the cash register.

At lunchtime, Scotty's is packed three deep at the bar with computer types from the industrial park picking up their phone-ordered hot sausage, hamburger, kolbassi or fish sandwiches with a side of fries and slaw. Scotty says that he doesn't need a three-page menu because everything he makes is the best.

Scotty's economic doctrine was proclaimed on a pair of signs above and behind him. One said, "Our Credit Manager is Helen Waite. If you need credit, go to Helen Waite." Its partner read, "We have an agreement with the bank- they don't serve drinks and we don't cash checks."

During evening rush hour the patrons are of the pocket-protector crowd who think the place has a certain appealing ambiance.

Unlike your run-of-the-mill cocktail lounge, Scotty's is brightly lighted with three banks of fluorescent lights so that the euchre and cribbage players can compete without straining their eyes. Scotty's wife,

Marie, says, "Dirt can't hide in the light, only in darkness." Marie DeGuerre is almost solely responsible for the antiseptic cleanliness of the place, though she refuses to enter the Men's Room.

White apron wrapped around his stocky girth at armpit level, Scotty was polishing some pilsner glasses when he noticed me and acknowledged my presence by nodding in my direction and saying, "PT." He set down the glass he was working on and poured me a Pepsi that he considerately garnished with a lime wedge. I acknowledged the transaction by sending some money his way and saying, "Scotty."

We weren't really deep conversationalists. I wended my way back to my habitual table towards the back and sat in such a way that I could see the TV, the front door, and the rest of the bar. A pair of elderly ladies nursing their sherry or Madeira in tall thin glasses guarded my back. The news was just coming on. A cute blonde talking head gave the headlines. Same as always: trouble in the Middle East, students rioting in Korea, the daily roll call of local shootings, something about the Pirates, the Penguins' search for a new igloo site and the weather teaser. I sipped at my drink and gave the afternoon Trib a once-over.

My Dad told me a long time ago that the headlines and the lead stories don't give you the news. The real news is in the business pages and in the legal notices. If you regularly read all the newsy little blurbs and announcements in the business pages, you'll be able to tell pretty much what was happening in and around town.

For instance, suppose that Joe James is vice president of shipping at ABC Company. Suddenly ABC Company is having all kinds of trouble with misdirected shipments, improperly packaged goods, and incorrect bills of lading. The company's stock drops. Before you know it, its competitor, DEF Company, pounces on ABC's customer base like a vulture. Next thing you know, and you can see it coming, Joe James is demoted and replaced by Sam Smith. End of story? No, keep reading the business pages. Six months later, there's a little notice saying that DEF Company is pleased to announce the appointment of Joe James to vice president of marketing or something. Now you know the real news.

A disagreement over serving policies taking place at the cash register brought me back to the present. Wild Willie Doyle was arguing with Scotty because Scotty wouldn't serve him.

"Ahhh come on Scotty, just one lousy beer for an out of work steelworker?" he implored while swaying before the bar.

"Naw, not tonight Willie. You've already had a snoot full," Scotty replied.

"Tell you what, though. I'll have Harry Sweeney give you a ride home. He's about ready to leave anyway."

Willie, all the while mumbling about how he wasn't going to stop here anymore once the mills started back up, slumped in a chair to wait for Harry. Marie scurried over to him with a steaming mug of black coffee.

I went back to my paper remembering something that my uncle once told me.

"Pedar," he said, "Never give coffee to someone who's drunk. All that's going to happen is that you are going to have a wide-awake drunk on your hands."

All the news on the front page and in the sports section that day was about the Penguins' search for a location to build a new hockey arena. Even though the mayor was from the North Side of the city, both the Pirates and the Steelers had just been presented with brand new stadiums on the North Side. It would be just too obvious if the new hockey arena should turn up on the North Side. Eliminate that area of the city from the list of possibilities. It had to be in the city though, because that's where most of the political hacks live.

Willie and Harry left the establishment, Willie hanging on Harry's left shoulder with his right arm draped over Harry's right shoulder. Willie was singing, "When the log rolls over, we will, die, we will die..." The door lumbered closed with its pneumatic assistant.

In the business pages of the Trib, I saw that Gummert Construction had just ordered three dozen pieces of heavy excavation equipment from Link Belt, Komatsu and Caterpillar. Now, I had been following this company for awhile and it appeared to be preparing for a major excavation and construction job. I knew, from keeping a watchful eye on the legal notices, that there were no big construction jobs coming up around the city that were waiting to be assigned. No big jobs were even near the bidding stages.

Somebody at Gummert Construction thought he was on to something. I also remember that a certain Kyle Snyder, prior assistant director of computer services for the city planning department, got a managerial position within the corporate spider web of Gummert Construction. Payback? Maybe.

I decided to keep an eye on Gummert. This company was definitely up to something.

Exie showed-up before I'd half-finished my Pepsi.

I knew he'd get the Scotsman – Scotty's Place reference.

He stopped at the bar and, glass of beer in hand, found his way back to me. He stopped in from of me and warned, "My man- you seem to have bitten off a wee bit more than you can chew. So what else is new?"

I rubbed a particularly tender spot in the vicinity of my left eye and agreed in principle, if not in fact.

"What's-up, Exie? How's the family?"

He squeezed his fit linebacker sized body into a chair catty-corner from me. That way, we both could indulge our healthy paranoia and observe all the comings and goings at the bar.

"Doing well. Young Seamus is having a blast in pee-wee football and Maria is always asking after you. That's not what I want to talk to you about." He ran his fingers through that blue black curly mess on top of his head and said, "You were involved in a traffic accident that escalated to aggravated assault and then murder, right?"

I wondered where this was going, folded the paper, and placed it to one side on the table top.

"Yeah, and?"

I wondered too, how the information about my, "Accident," had filtered through the police grapevine so quickly.

Those blue Irish eyes of his weren't smiling now.

"Does it seem just the littlest bit unusual that the same pair of city dicks that investigate accidents also investigate murders?"

That's it! That's what had been nagging at my subconscious. Guys who investigate car wrecks are either just starting out or are burnt out. Murder investigators are the cream of the crop.

In a city the size of Pittsburgh, the sheer size of the police department bureaucracy would prevent someone from doing both jobs.

I gave myself a light smack on the forehead with the hell of my hand and said, "Little Cricket has seen the sunrise Master O'Reilly. What gives?"

"Have you ever heard of The Independents?"

I replied, "No. Do you want a refill?"

I got a new Pepsi for me and a new draught for him and sat down back at the table. Exie spent the next half-hour telling me about this special police department within a police department. They were an off-shoot of Internal Investigations, that Judas group of detectives whose only job was to investigate fellow officers and make mountainous charges out of mole hill transgressions. Investigators from outside the department catch the real bad apples.

These men reported to no one. They came under the aegis of the mayor's office. Their job was to conduct operations that hizzoner's office took interest in. Like digging-up dirt on political foes, for instance.

"OK, what you are telling me is that Shallenberger and Todd are members of this group."

He paused to wipe a beer foam mustache from his upper lip before replying.

"Yep, that's it. And these folk aren't famous for sticking to rules, or the rule of law, for that matter."

Then, with all the earnestness that he could muster, he said, "Seriously, watch your back. I'd tell you to lay off if I thought it would do any good. I know better."

He finished his beer and placed the mug on the table while sliding his chair back.

He concluded by saying, "And, PT, don't trust your phones. If you need me, call me from somewhere else. Or use your cell phone. I'll be there for you."

With that we parted ways, each assuring the other that we'd get together again soon, and not for business.

The short walk back to the office along the storm scoured sidewalk cleared my mind a bit. If all it took was a thorough cleaning to make the city look and smell this fresh, maybe there was hope after all.

So I tidied up my desk, shut down my computer, and went out the back way to pick up one of the company cars for the ride home feeling optimistic.

On the way home I think I kept seeing the same pair of headlights in my rear view mirror. I chalked it up to Exie's getting me hinky with all his talk about secret police forces. So much for optimism.

# CHAPTER 7 – DANNY THE DUDE

Tuesday. It's amazing what a good night's sleep can do for a person's outlook. I woke up with fewer aches, pains and creaking joints than I took to bed. It probably had something to do with Beth's ministrations.

She returned to Pittsburgh on a TransAir flight from Chicago at 8:00PM and came directly to my place. When she saw that my injuries had confined themselves to a bunch of bruises and scrapes, she showed her relief by giving me a gentle head-to-toe rub down. She had me sleeping like a baby in no time and she went home. Tendrils of her musky perfume hinted of her presence when I awoke.

I met her one morning during my morning run along the rails to trails path by the Monongahela River. She was also running, about a hundred yards ahead of me when three young toughs accosted her, one of whom brandished a knife.

I switched from my distance-covering lope to a sprint in order to come to her assistance. However, by the time I got to her side, two of the three were running in fear of their lives while the third was writhing on the ground at her feet wailing about his broken right forearm.

I scooped one of the runaways up by his waistband and helped him walk back to her by utilizing the universal come-along hold. That's the one your mother and mine used on us as kids. Simply grasp a handful of ear and lift. Your prisoner will now go in any direction his ear goes.

Slightly flushed with a healthy glow and her rather adequate breasts heaving with the exertion, she certainly did not need my help.

"…And, if you even think about getting up, I'll break your other arm."

She must've caught my approach out of the corner of her eyes because she spun in my direction holding the knife she had confiscated from the young thug. Seeing that I had one of the other two miscreants in tow, she lowered her guard and commented, "You should've let him run. Now we'll have to deal with both of them."

She got on her cell phone and made all the necessary arrangements with the city police. The medics arrived first and started treating the young punk's broken arm. On their heels the police arrived and took our statements. One of them looked unbelieving at Beth and the other looked disdainfully at me as we explained that it was Beth who disarmed o0ne thug and sent the other two running before I could even get to the scene. Then they took the malefactors in tow and departed saying that someone would be in touch.

As they headed back to their patrol car, I overheard one say to the other, "I sure hope my wife doesn't learn any of that kung fu crap."

The other officer muttered agreement.

That was two years ago. We both have careers that tend to make us less than confident in the good will of other humans, (she's a family law attorney), so our friendship has grown slowly. I think that's the best way because now we have a deep understanding of one another each acknowledging our love for the other as a whole person, including flaws. I got the better of that deal, having a lot more flaws.

Anyhow, her rejuvenation therapy worked wonders. Maybe I'll be able to hit the gym for a workout tonight or tomorrow.

I also woke up famished and nothing in the 'fridge was even remotely appealing. Shaved, showered, dressed and drove the company heap to a quaint old place in Southside called the Terminal Diner. I wasn't in the mood for anything healthful, so I ordered a stack of pancakes, a double order of sausage, a mound of home fries and some strong coffee.

For some reason, probably just morbid curiosity and the fact that the diner was located nearby, I drove across the Tenth Street Bridge to the other side of the river, turned right on Second Avenue and drove the two miles upstream to the location of my, "Accident." After satisfying myself that a construction site is a construction site is a construction site, I drove back across the river via the Birmingham Bridge at that location and traveled the mile or so distance to check if Unk's scrap yard was still there. It was. I headed to the other side of the Monongahela River where our office is located.

I parked the car in the fenced-in back and, since it wasn't blistering hot yet, walked around and entered the building through the front doors. I Blew Pamula a kiss on the way by and got to my desk before nine-thirty: nice start.

First things first: I brewed some of my special blend of coffee and got a nice steaming mug of it to sip while I checked the day's newspapers. Mainly I just skimmed the headlines and lead stories to see if anything pertinent to our business happened overnight.

Next I ran through the mail, which Pamula is gracious enough to place on my desk's upper left-hand corner each morning. It was the usual. There was a life insurance offer especially for veterans, relatives of veterans, or people who once knew a veteran. Next were a couple of credit card offers, a few chances to refinance my nonexistent house at today's low interest rates, and the inescapable no-obligation magazine subscriptions.

However, there was one small white envelope that caught my attention. It sported no return address. I opened it and it contained five playing cards in the form of a poker hand: two pair- aces over eights.

Then I tackled the email that tends to clog my computer on a daily basis. After determining that I wanted modifications to neither my manhood nor my bust size, that liaisons with any of a variety of sex-starved damsels was not my idea of true love, and that my medicine cabinet was adequately stocked; I found a couple of useful messages that my anti-virus and firewall programs permitted me to read.

The mail out of the way, I helped myself to another steaming mug and settled in for a long bout with the phone and computer. I needed to learn everything there was to know about Danny Saint Martin, his businesses, associates, employees, likes, dislikes, favorite foods and foibles. The Internet is a wonderful thing. Armed with nothing more than a good search engine and a subject, I found torrent of information. Since I have ways to gain access to credit reporting and government databases, I hit the mother lode.

When I was finished a couple of hours later, that poker hand was still nagging me. I had to report to Will anyway, so I dropped in on him.

He was obviously involved in something intricate. Papers were covering nearly every square inch of his desk. He looked up, saw me, and said, "What's up?"

I made as though to go, but he swept the papers to one side, clearing the deck so-to-speak, asking, "How's the case looking from your end?" He didn't have to indicate which case.

I crossed the room, placed my notes on one of the chairs facing his desk and handed him the envelope containing the playing cards.

"What do you make of this, Will?"

He extracted the cards from the envelope, fanned them out in his hand and placed them on his desk facing himself.

"Aces over eights: the dead man's hand. Legend has it that Wild Bill

Hickock was holding this hand when he was shot in the back in the town of Deadwood, South Dakota."

Will looked up and me and continued, "Whoever sent you this must know their western stories. You'll notice that the fifth card is the five of diamonds. The five of diamonds is supposedly the actual fifth card and is on display in the saloon at Deadwood, South Dakota."

I was grateful for the lesson in Nineteenth Century American History, but my interest in the cards was more contemporary in nature, and I said so.

Will explained, "For a while in the early 1900s, gangsters used to send this poker hand as both a warning and a means of intimidation to people who were interfering with them."

He put them back into the envelope and tossed it back to me, saying, "Looks like someone is trying to intimidate you. Do you feel intimidated?"

"No. Pissed is more like it." I mentally set it aside for later cogitation.

I took a swallow of my coffee, put the mug down and picked up my notes.

"I learned a ton about our Mr. Danny Saint Martin. Want to hear it?"

Will nodded. I rearranged a couple of pages and started in, "For starters, he changed his name from Dante Santa Marianna a dozen years ago. His petition listed the reason as wishing to avoid the prejudice associated with an obviously ethnic name."

Will's chin rested on his tented fingers and a look of intense concentration was on his face. However, it seemed that he was directing his concentration behind me and not on what I was saying.

I tried to go on. "Data from the major credit reporting agencies have given me his addresses going back fifteen years and has shown me the bills he has paid as well as those he hasn't."

It was no good. I didn't have Will's attention. I looked over my shoulder to see what had his attention and I saw it. I got out of my chair and went to the opposite wall where there was a new addition to his collection of maritime artifacts: a brass-bound wooden ship's wheel.

"Wow- where'd this come from?"

The pride in his voice was evident as he told me more than I cared to know about this particular ship's wheel. He explained that it was from an early 1800s whaler out of Fall River, Mass. called the Eliza Marie and that it had taken him three years to track it down.

He got out from behind his desk and came over to the wheel and showed me where the hub was darkened from many years of greasing it with whale blubber.

"Look here, PT. You can even see where the spokes have worn from the times the wheel was lashed in place when the helmsman was needed elsewhere."

I made myself suitably awestricken concerning his latest acquisition and eventually got him back behind his desk and concentrating on the matter at hand.

I picked-up where I had left off. "Saint Martin has platinum credit cards from all the major credit card companies, even though his occupation is listed as manager of the Regis J. McKinley Reading Society with an income of less than forty thousand dollars annually."

Will smiled and said, "Sounds like our boy is just a tad over extended."

I agreed and said, "Yeah. If he only makes forty grand a year. He has a mortgage on his Point Breeze home of over a quarter million dollars. The payments alone on that are nearly fifteen thou' a year."

Will started doodling on his sketch pad. That's when I knew I had his full attention. I finished that page of notes saying, "He's got car loans of over a hundred thousand as well as revolving lines of credit at various haberdashers, furnishing outlets, department stores and sporting goods stores. He even owes money to a number of high end women's clothing outlets and jewelers. For crying out loud: his total payments are more than what he reports as income. And everything is up-to-date!"

Will looked up, said, "Maybe he has a Fairy God Mother," and went back to his doodling.

I rolled my eyes for no one's benefit other than my own and continued with my recitation, "I checked the local newspaper archives and found his various marriage license applications as well as his divorce decrees. Add paid-up alimony to his yearly disbursements."

I don't care how comfy a chair is, you sit long enough and your butt is going to start protesting. I got up and leaned on the corner of Will's desk while I went on, "He applied for and was granted a license to operate the Regis J. McKinley Reading Society and Benevolent Association by transferring a defunct club license that he had purchased a few years back."

I put those pages of notes on the corner of the desk where I had been leaning and started moving around his office while referring to the next batch of notes.

"By cross-referencing his birth name with his legal name, I found that his mother, Consuela Francesa Santa Marianna is listed as the president and CEO of R. R. Smith Aggregate and Paving."

As I passed the front of Will's desk for the, I don't know, third or fourth time, he looked-up and said, "Would you please find a place to perch?"

So much for my sore butt. I sat down.

"OK, R. R. Smith is a concrete and asphalt supply company that also supplies concrete casting forms to the construction trade. It has a workforce of two hundred and is at the top of the list of preferred contractors when any major construction or roadwork is attempted in and around the city."

Will set aside his pencil for a few moments while he interjected, "You know, concrete is one of those things we see without seeing. Whenever any municipality starts a renewal project, whenever a holding company erects a shopping mall, wherever roads or bridges are built or rebuilt: a tremendous amount of it is necessary. Think about it." He went back to his sketch pad.

A glimmer of the connection between Danny Saint Martin and Unk's scrap yard on the South Side was making itself felt, albeit subconsciously.

Having brought Will up to date with my morning findings, I took leave of his office. I couldn't resist a parting shot, "Well now there's two big wheels in this office."

As the door closed behind me, he looked up from his desk and deadpanned, "Huh?"

Time for a late lunch. I walked over to Scotty's and had a Reuben with slaw and a tall iced tea. I looked over the morning paper and found that during the night someone had painted the panthers at either end of the Panther Hollow Bridge pink. Kids. Sure beats the profanity-laden graffiti found on nearly every other accessible surface in the city.

Not a lot in the business section. Disney had ordered yet another cruise ship. This expenditure might cause its stock to go down a bit, making it a good buy until the ship went into operation and started making money. Any time Disney stock is down it's a good buy. Here was another tip: National Can Corp. had just nearly doubled its steel order. At the same time Conklin Brewing was advertising for brewery workers, administrative staff, and truck drivers. This indicated to the trained eye that Conklin Brewing was planning a major sales event in a couple of months. If a person had some loose change, both Conklin and National might be good short-term investments.

On the other hand, if the sales event fell flat, they could both tank.

I also saw where Universal Steel was upping its structural steel output. Not much, only five percent. Even so, that was a lot of steel.

Lunch is never leisurely. It was time to get back to the office and do some follow-up.

I spent some more time tracing Danny Saint Martin's money trail and decided that someone somewhere was going to a lot of trouble to keep him out of the IRS's cross-hairs. Nobody could live the way he had been living without attracting some unwanted attention from the tax boys.

Mid-afternoon brought yet another visit from the Detectives, Shallenberger and Todd.

It was too late in the day for coffee, so they helped themselves to something cold and non-alcoholic from my wet bar. Todd was his usual colorless self while Shallenberger resembled nothing less than a side show barker. Everything he wore clashed with everything else he wore. The only thing missing was the cane.

Shallenberger tossed his straw hat on one of my chairs, sat down in another one, crossed his legs, drank appreciatively from whatever he had in his glass and said, "Just stopped by to see if you wanted to add anything to what you told us yesterday?" Shallenberger was being nice. That, added to Exie's warning, put me on guard.

Shallenberger wanted me to go over the night of the murder again, in detail, to see if there was anything that I had, "forgotten."

"The boys at forensics called to say that they found no evidence of window glass in or on the clothing you were wearing at the time of your unfortunate incident." This from Todd. I had nearly forgotten about him. He tends to fade into the background when Shallenberger is at center stage. That made him dangerous in my book.

"Yeah," Shallenberger chipped in, "That's unusual when the driver's side window is blown in."

He accompanied this last with a smile reminiscent of a snake hypnotizing a mouse.

I smiled, "Just lucky, I guess."

Todd said, "Let's hope your luck holds out.

It was nearly four when, as they were leaving, Todd tossed over his shoulder, "Funny thing. A set of clothes found in one of the concrete forms seem to be your size. There were bits and pieces of glass all over them."

I felt threatened.

I didn't feel like ending my day at Scotty's and felt less like going straight home, so I called Beth and asked her if I could pick her brains while she picked at some food.

There is an excellent little sidewalk café off the beaten path in the Shadyside section of the city. The food is superb, the ambiance quietly eclectic and the youthful staff makes each patron feel as though they were the only customer.

Even though The Café had a hefty corking fee, I brought a 2001 Robert Mondavi Chardonnay. It was a wine of a particularly fine vintage that went with anything.

I arrived a bit before Beth. Her schedule as a battered women's and children's advocate is often as unsure as my own. For this reason we often arrange to meet somewhere with flexibility built in to the arrangement.

The muted thunder of her 1968 electric blue 427 AC/Cobra Roadster heralded her arrival. Beth was like her car. They both made heads turn, especially male ones. She was a five foot nine, one hundred thirty-five pound, auburn-haired Irish-Italian beauty that was the white race's answer to Pamula. I watched her walk through the entrance and straight to our table. I rose to greet her. There's just something about long legs, short skirts and that damn reddish brown hair. I don't know what it is, but it sure works for me. On second thought, I do know what it is.

"Sorry I'm late," she said, "I had a last minute Protection From Abuse order to get approved so some asshole would stay away from his wife at least long enough for her current bruises to heal."

I got up. We exchanged hugs and kisses and I held her chair for her as she made her perfect little rump comfortable.

"No problem, hon. I just beat you by a couple of minutes."

Following the suggestions of our waitress we started our dinner with a cold cantaloupe and mint soup with strawberry crème fraiche. For an appetizer, the chef had constructed a smoked salmon and avocado mousse with caramelized pineapple en crostine.

We didn't want anything to interfere with our enjoyment of food of this caliber, so we kept dinner conversation on the light side.

For an entrée, Beth selected the grilled sockeye salmon with roasted tomato and olive ragout, accompanied by sun dried tomato and parmesan polenta and grilled asparagus.

I had the pork loin medallion stuffed with mango and jalapeno on a bed of wilted mustard greens and a side of roasted plantains. Our bread was a warm crusty baguette slathered with roasted shallot and chive butter.

After this kind of a meal we were tempted to pass on the dessert, but the chef, Ambrose by name, would have none of it. He insisted that we have a light dessert of his selection. It was passion fruit crème brulee which consists of delicate passion fruit custard with caramelized sugar.

The arrival of our espressos signaled the end of an excellent dinner and the start of important conversation.

She ran the tip of her tongue across her upper lip to clear it of the froth from the espresso and said, "Have you figured out why Saint Martin's men have a thing for the scrap yard?"

I returned my cup to its saucer, "Well Beth, it's like this…"

I went on for a full ten minutes telling her all I learned about Danny, his life and times. Then I told her about Exie's warning concerning Shallenberger and those damn pesky threats showing up on my answering machine. When I mentioned the 'Dead Man's Hand", she rolled her eyes and said something about the theatricality of it.

"Poor guy – it sure sounds like your dance card is punched", the worry evident in her eyes belied the sarcasm.

She put her brain to work and I could imagine tiny little electrical impulses racing through a myriad of silicon chip circuit boards in that fabulous brain of hers inside that equally beautiful face of hers.

"Hon," she said, "I hate to leave you in the dark, but I'll need a day or so to digest what you've told me. I want to do some cross-checking on my own. Off hand, it sounds like you're trying to fit pieces from one puzzle into another."

Nothing to do but wait. No amount of cajoling would get anything out of Beth until she was one hundred percent sure of her answer.

She did throw a morsel my way by saying, "Danny Saint Martin – Mrs. Santa Marianna – R.R. Smith Company – You were found in a concrete form at a construction site – are any bells ringing?"

I very generously paid the tab with a company credit card since of course, it was technically a business dinner.

We enjoyed the summer evening by walking off our dinner the few blocks to Shadyside proper where we had a light cocktail before walking back to our cars near the café. She insisted that I pay for the cocktails out of pocket, telling me that she didn't consider a summer stroll to be a business expense.

She actually seemed upset that I paid for our dinner with a company card. Sometimes even the most practical of women get weird.

Whatever, I returned home around eleven. There were two messages on my machine.

The first, from Exie, informed me that the phone number I gave him to trace came back to a pay phone at Monroeville Mall.

The second was another threat.

I went to bed alone.

# CHAPTER 8 – A QUIET DAY

Finally, a day to get some work done. There were neither any unannounced nor unwelcome visits from the minions of the law. By ten o'clock I had scanned the newspaper and opened and read my mail. I had already consumed my second cup of coffee and was starting to pay attention to some long-neglected paperwork.

I wish real life was like movies and TV. I have never seen an investigator in the movies or on TV do any paperwork. In real life it's 75 percent of the job. Another thing that gets me: I've never seen a TV cop fill out an overtime slip for all those extra hours. While I'm at it: Why do TV detectives always get a parking spot right in front of where they're going?

I worked straight through on the keyboard, transcribing all my notes from last week into a coherent package that would satisfy Will, printed one copy, and saved the file to disc. This took four hours, so I ran over to Scotty's for a quick sandwich and an iced tea, getting back to the office at two-thirty.

"Will wants to see you in his office," said Pamula.

I wondered what he'd been up to, since I hadn't seen him all day. I popped a stick of gum into my mouth and entered Will's office, taking my usual chair second from the right.

The big guy was on the phone. While he conversed with someone from the local Chamber of Commerce about sponsoring a Little League Team, I let his desk speak to me. My ancestors weren't all that thrilled about coming to America. Between the potato blight and the caprice of the people in power, it was a choice: starve to death or immigrate.

I honestly think that Will's ancestors would have willingly starved to death rather than face what was in store for them in the so-called Land of Opportunity. I wondered how much death, spilled blood and outright torture that slab of wood has witnessed.

He finished his conversation, broke the connection and replaced the phone in its cradle.

"I guess you've been wondering where I've been all day," he said, breaking into my morbid reverie.

"No, not really," I lied, "I've kept myself fairly busy catching up on things."

"Whatever. I've been Downtown to see a friend in the DA's office." Will went on to explain that, in light of Shallenberger and Todd's accusations, he was concerned about the firm's position vis-à-vis the legal branch of local government.

When a person spends as long as Will in this business, he tends to make friends and enemies in both low and high places. Along the way he has done many favors for people with long memories. When the time comes, those people are eager to repay the favor. That's the way it was at the district attorney's office. More of the ADA's (Assistant DAs) have had cases solidified through Will's efforts than have had them torpedoed.

"I had a relaxing and informative luncheon with the ADA in charge of Capital Prosecutions."

He didn't have to mention names we both knew who he was speaking of.

I shifted my piece of gum to an out of the way place between my cheek and molars and mentioned my cold sandwich at Scotty's. He commiserated by saying that at least, I didn't have to wear a suit coat and a noose around my neck to eat. He had me there.

He kept talking, "As you know, most of what the detectives were threatening was absolute B.S. There isn't even any thought being given to charges of evidence tampering, by us or anyone else."

He skewered me with a look of mock intensity and intoned, "You however, are suspect numero uno point one until somebody better comes along."

"Why point one?" I asked.

He smiled, "Because our friend Mr. Armand Mosticello is suspect numero uno. It's just that, for some reason or another, he seems to have taken a powder."

"Yeah," I interjected, "like a healthy concern for his own well-being."

"Anyway," Will said, "I promised that ADA that, if we located the elusive Mr. Mosticello, I would drop her a dime."

I wisely refrained from telling Will that phone calls haven't cost a dime in decades.

By the time we digested all Will had learned, it was quitting time.

Physically I felt pretty good, so I decided to have a workout at the gym.

I took a company car and headed for McKees Rocks. The tail end of rush hour didn't make it a Sunday drive in the country, but neither did it make it miserable. Like anyone from this area, I knew a few shortcuts that enabled me to go right through the heart of the city without undue delay. The approach to the Fort Pitt Bridge ramps heading south on Carson Street was backed-up. Being stalled a few moments in the stop-and-go traffic afforded me a view of Pittsburgh's Golden Triangle, one of the country's more spectacular cityscapes. The PPG building's towers caught the evening sun in such a way that it looked like a misplaced ice castle.

The Golden Triangle is the face that the city likes to put forth. A half mile south of the Fort Pitt Bridge, everything returns to the brown and grey of grit, dust and despair. The buildings no longer glisten in the evening shadows. Instead, they try to hide in those shadows as though ashamed of what they have become.

In order to get to the bottoms section of McKees Rocks I had to drive through a forbidding area of rusted-out factories that is criss-crossed with overgrown railroad tracks. This in turn gave way to an area of sparkling clean little brick homes reminiscent of the row houses of Lawrenceville. Here however, the houses are individual units separated by a three-foot wide alleyway and each one has a ten by twenty front yard and a back yard. These homes were originally built by middle European immigrants who came to the area during two world wars both to escape their ravaged homelands and because of the readily available jobs in the heavy industry of the area.

Right smack in the middle of the bottoms is where Jim located his gym. Unlike your typical health club where dilettantes, divorcees and muscle men go to impress one another and find true love, Jim's Gym was physically just a gym. What made it more than a gym was Jim Shepherd.

Jim Shepherd was a retired county cop with an affinity for two things: boxing and kids. His rapport with kids was legendary. Once as punishment for some imagined transgression against department policy (he offended a politician) he found himself reassigned to traffic control at a busy crosswalk as a uniformed officer. In his first week at that crosswalk, he made so many narcotics arrests, *while in uniform*, due to his network of teenage informants that it necessitated his reassignment back to the detective division. Otherwise, the uniformed division would have needed another officer on a full-time basis just to cover for him on his court dates.

Then there was the time that Jim was assigned undercover narcotics work. After months of investigation and undercover buys, warrants were issued for the arrest of some twenty-seven people for drug law violations.

All of these warrants were because of Jim's investigations.

Because the perpetrators were considered armed, dangerous and unpredictable, a number of combined uniformed and detective teams executed the round-up at five in the morning. Experience has shown that ne'er-do-wells are at their lowest ebb this hour of the morning.

Jim went along with one of the arrest teams and, after the arrests, rode in the back of the wagon with the suspects. He spent the entire forty minute trip back to the county lock-up trying to explain to the six suspects that they had certain guaranteed constitutional rights. They refused to believe that he was an officer and kept asking how he had gotten out of his hand cuffs.

One of them, a mid-level pusher, kept exhorting him to, "Stop fooling around, we're in some deep shit and better get our stories straight."

When Jim went to the officer's entrance and checked-in his firearm was the first that anyone of them would believe that he was a cop. Then, instead of feeling angry, hurt or betrayed, they all congratulated him on his expertise as an undercover operative

Stories about this character have become legend on the force.

To say that Jim was unconventional is failure to do justice to his individuality.

Anyhow, after his retirement he had found a storefront in the McKees Rocks Bottoms near the river. With a lot of work and some borrowed money, he transformed it into Jim's Gym. Although there were enough paying members like me to cover the rent and utilities, the bulk of the gym's membership was nonpaying kids from various parts of the city that Jim had rescued from the street.

These kids were imbued with Jim's refreshingly old-fashioned credo. The way to fulfillment is in a clean, healthy body and a clean, healthy mind. You never tell a lie and you never turn down a friend in need. Oh, and you give everyone the respect that they deserve while demanding that you deserve their respect in turn.

The net result of this was that, in a few years, most of the area's Golden Gloves champions were polite, soft-spoken, confident kids from Jim's Gym.

I got there around five, changed into a well-seasoned grey sweat suit, and headed for the ring area.

No fancy stationary bikes, treadmills or stair climbers here. Ten minutes with a jump rope gave me all the cardio warm-up I needed.

Then it was over to the free weights for a half hour that worked just about every muscle in my body. No Nautilus, BowFlex or SoloFlex here, just cast-iron weights. If you really need a workout on a bicycle, Jim'll loan you one and point you out the door. If you want to do a few laps around the pool, he'll give you directions to the nearest Y. Instead of a treadmill, Jim uses the byways, sidewalks and foot paths of the Bottoms.

After a 40 minute workout I was drenched with sweat and gladly hit the showers. Ten minutes later with a scalding shower behind me, I put on street clothes, got a Pepsi from the machine, and walked over to the boxing ring.

Two youngsters, about fifteen or sixteen, wearing padded gloves and headgear were dancing around one another and throwing half-hearted punches. A group of about a dozen boys in boxing shorts hung around the ring kibitzing and giving pointers.

"Come on, Carlos, jab, jab, jab. Don't wave your arms."

"Mikey, if you punch any nearer to him, the wind will knock him down."

"You must be Dutch because you love windmilling."

Those who knew that their turn was just around the corner offered lots of other good-natured advice and ribbing.

One thing that was conspicuous by its absence: profanity. Jim can't abide it, calling it the mark of an intellectual midget.

I walked over to Jim to say hi, and he told me that these two clumsy kids could take just about anybody apart. That is, if they had knives instead of gloves. But, he said that his chief trainer and early success story, Reynaldo Hayes, would soon have both their footwork and glove work in order. Then he took me aside and both his voice and expression exhibited concern.

"A few of my boys have told me that you are sailing into stormy waters. Here at the gym we have a saying, 'friends don't let friends die young.' You are a friend. 'nough said."

Cryptic remarks not withstanding, the workout had done its job. I was both refreshed and relaxed. I called it a night.

*

Did you ever notice that Thursday is pretty much of a nothing day? Monday starts the workweek. Tuesday has you pretty much into the swing of things. Wednesday is hump day, when you are fully into the work ethic and a lot gets accomplished. Friday involves a lot of rushing around to finish as much as possible before the end of the week. Saturday is when all the household chores get attention and Saturday night is play time. Sunday is reserved for worship, reflection, and rest.

That leaves Thursday, Drudge Day. You go through the motions, but it's too late in the week to start anything new. Friday is still to come, so there's a whole 'nother day to wrap things up.

That's Thursday. Will suggested I get a replacement for the car I had totaled. Since city driving is the bulk of the mileage I put on a car, I got myself a nicely optioned-out mid size sedan with power everything. This would make it easier to maneuver through narrow, twisting city streets with barely enough space to pass another car head-on. I had it fitted with a built-in, hands-free cell phone and a global positioning system in the dash. I also got a transmitting GPS units slaved to the one in the dash: Good bye to lost tails. For those times I might be in a hurry, it also had a remote starter. The ignition had a digital lockout that needed a pass code before the car would start.

As a concession to my baser instincts, I ordered the most powerful engine available, a muffler to make that engine sound like a one-lunger, and an oversize fuel tank. I got it in the most innocuous, fade-into-the-background puke green paint job imaginable.

The dealer said it would be ready in about a week and would cost as much as a Mercedes.

I drove back in the company car and lunched at Scotty's.

The Pirates were playing a home game that night against the Indians, an intra-league game. I was able to score a couple of free tickets, so I called Detective Sergeant Xavier O'Reilly from a pay phone and we took in the ball game. I was kind of hoping it would be as exciting as the Steelers-Browns rivalry during football season. I guess it was- for die hard baseball fans. It was a real pitchers' duel. Final score being Pittsburgh: one, Cleveland: zero.

Be that as it may, Exie took this opportunity to fill me in more completely concerning the Independents.

When I returned home, a crude skull and crossbones spray painted on my front door indicated that someone thought my presence was toxic to their intentions.

Today's message on my answering machine simply said, "We know where you live." I wondered how, "They," found out where I lived.

The time markers in my answering machine indicated that the earliest threat came at 3:35PM and the latest at 11:45PM. All had originated from various shopping malls in the area with the exception of the one at 11:45PM. That one was from a pay phone at a gas station located across the road from a miniature golf course in Monroeville, not all that far from the mall. I was able to get these locations with the help of my Caller ID and Exie's connections.

I hope that whoever is doing this, and I have my suspicions, is not counting on scaring me.

I don't react well to intimidation.

# CHAPTER 9 – FREAKY FRIDAY

Some days you just wish you stayed in bed. This was one of them.

As soon as I walked in the office, before I even got a mug of coffee, before I even got to my office, Pamula told me to see Will ASAP.

The instant I entered his office Will picked up a document with a pair of ice tongs and set it facing me.

"What do you make of this, PT?"

It was a classic extortion letter like the ones you see on TV, made up of words cut from various magazines and arranged to make a statement:

"Junk Man. I have had it with you. The game is over. You are a dead man."

I turned it over with the tongs and examined the note. The paper seemed to have come from a brown paper bag. I had never seen nor heard of a note like this outside of an old B movie or a less than imaginative TV show.

"Uncle Clarence found this note slipped under his door when he opened up this morning. He brought it straight to me. PT, this crap has got to cease. It's time to pressure Mr. Saint Martin."

Will got up and came around his desk close to me. He sat on the edge of the desk facing me, and enunciating every work with intensity, gave me explicit instructions:

"Pay him a visit and insure that he understands that we are taking this personally. Make sure that he understands that it is in his *own personal best* interest that Uncle Clarence suffer not so much as a broken finger nail."

"OK, Will. I'll see to it."

As I headed out of his office, Will called me back with, "Oh, PT: try not to make too much of a scene this time, OK?"

I gave him my promise that I would try, for whatever it was worth, and went to my office, brewed a pot of my special blend and settled down with a steaming mug to peruse the paper and mail. The intercom buzzed.

"PT, Nick is here to see you."

"Thanks Pamula. Send him on in."

A few second later my door swung open and one agitated operative barged in. Without a word he strode to my wet bar, helped himself to a glass of ice that he poured root beer over and plopped himself down in one of the arm chairs facing my desk.

Hanging his right leg over the arm of the chair, he swallowed a bit of his drink and said, "PT, something crazy is going on with this Locke woman. It would be easier to keep track of Big Foot and his extended family than her."

I stared longingly over his shoulder at my, "Wall of shame," collection of kayak paddles broken whilst running various rapids. This felt like it was going to be an involved story.

"In what way, Nick," I innocently inquired.

"Damned if I know," He replied, "I have utterly and completely lost her every single day since I started this job. Moreover, I don't think she even knows that she's being tailed."

Nicholas Moore is the finest operative in the city of Pittsburgh. His accomplishments are legendary. In fact, he once stayed on the tail of a bookie's runner around that guy's entire route without having been discovered or shaken off the trail. Any vice cop can tell you a bookie's runner is the hardest person in the world to tail. For Nick to lose a subject three days in a row was inconceivable.

Inconsolable dejection was evident in both his bearing and his expression as he continued, "I started off first thing Tuesday morning by parking a ways up the road from their house where I could see the entrance to the Locke's driveway."

No relaxing reveries about past whitewater trips were to be in store for me today. I got another mug of coffee and grunted something meant to encourage Nick to go on. He did.

"After a while, a metallic blue Jag XJ coupe came blasting out of the drive with a blonde at the wheel. As the Jag sped by me, I got a good look at the driver and she pretty well matched the picture of Vivien Locke that you gave me. I gave her a few seconds, then did a U-turn and followed."

I set my mug down on an old mouse pad that I use as a coaster and commented, "So far, so good. It sounds routine. What happened?"

"Well, she drove right out of Fox Chapel like she was on a mission for God. Took the turnpike east from the Allegheny Valley Interchange to the Monroeville Interchange and went straight to Monroeville Mall.

"As luck would have it, she got a spot almost next to the Sears Entrance and went in. I got a spot a hundred feet away and kept her pretty much in sight 'til she entered the building. I swear that I wasn't more'n a few seconds behind her, but I couldn't find her anywhere inside. She just walked through those damn doors and disappeared."

I tried to be supportive by saying, "OK, it happens. What next?"

He shifted in the chair trying to get more comfortable. He switched legs and draped his left over the other arm of the chair. He looked over my shoulder at the huge photo of Sweet's Falls that dominates the wall behind my desk.

"I went back to my car and kept watch on the Jag. I figured that she had just slipped into one of those mall Boat-tee-cues and would be out with an armload of bags soon. Boy was I wrong. Thank God for air conditioning!"

He swallowed some more root beer, cleared his throat and went on, "By four in the afternoon, I'd burned a half-tank of gas idling. I got restless and decided to walk around the mall hoping to catch a glimpse of her. When I returned to my car, her Jag was gone. So, I high-tailed it back to Fox Chapel and got there just in time to see the turn signal of the Jag make known its intention to enter the Locke's driveway."

By know it was obvious, at least to Nick, that he wasn't going to get comfortable in one of my chairs. He got up, refreshed his root beer and started pacing the office from side to side in front of my desk.

"I thought that she might be going out again since her hubby wasn't due for a while yet. So I waited."

I felt as though I were watching a tennis match as he seemed to carom from wall to wall and kept talking.

"Then, about six-thirty, her husband's car came up the road and who do you think was with him?"

I knew the question was rhetorical, so I stayed mum.

"Her! That's who!

"So I packed it in for the day and went across the bridge to a spot on the Allegheny River Boulevard for dinner."

I tried to assuage the damage to his professional pride by explaining to him that it was just a fluke and these things happen to everyone at one time or another. He countered by telling me that it never, never happens to him.

"OK, how about Wednesday?" I asked.

He paused in his pacing long enough to get started with the account of that day.

"I got to the house early on and set up a surveillance on the drive. A cab entered the drive around nine and came out a minute later with her in it. I felt better right off because there's nothing easier to tail than a taxi."

Nick? Pick a spot and settle. All of your running around is giving me a crick in the neck."

"Huh?" he said, unaware that he'd been pacing, "Sorry." He sat down again and continued.

"The cab took pretty much the same route as she did on Tuesday. I vowed that I would leave my car right smack in the middle of the road, if I had to, to keep her in sight."

Nick then gave a tortuous travelogue of the eastern suburbs of Pittsburgh, finally arriving at Bouquet Airport, a little grass strip near Delmont.

He got up and leaned on my desk, both of his large hands grasping the edge as he nearly yelled, "By the time I got out of my car, she was in a Cessna 172 taxiing to the runway. She must've called ahead and had the pilot and plane warmed-up and ready to go. I was just in time to watch the plane achieve rotation and take off."

He sat down again and rested his right elbow on the arm of the chair and his forehead on his right hand. I couldn't quite figure out why he was so upset. After all it was just a simple tail, wasn't it?

He intoned, "Another day down the tubes, right? I went back to Fox Chapel and waited. And waited. About six-fifteen the husband's Caddy came up the road, and ten-to-one you can guess who was sitting pretty right next to him."

"Alright already. It's just a simple tail."

I picked up my mug to drink some coffee, thought better of it and placed it back down.

Nick looked up at me and said, "Maybe to you it's a simple tail. To me it's an insult to my ability.

"Anyhow, I went back across the river for some beer and sandwiches. You know, this job is going to either make me a beeraholic or a fatty."

I gave Nick my solemn assurance that nobody, not even he, can be prepared for a subject to sprout wings and disappear into the afternoon sky.

"After all," I asked, "Do you have a chopper in your trunk?"

His reply was short and explicit.

Unfortunately, I took this chance to sip at my coffee. Before I knew what was happening, I was being entertained with a scene by scene account of how Nick tried to diminish his sense of failure through wine, women and debauchery. In certain circles, this ex-athlete was famous for all three.

"...and then we went to the Harlequin Room at the Wooden Wine Jug."

He paused to wet his whistle with some root beer.

"Nick? Nick? NICK! What about Thursday?"

"I don't want to talk about it."

I'd just about had it with his whining. I wanted results.

"Yeah, well I don't give a rat's posterior. You're on my dime and my clock and I want to hear about it."

"Are you sure? OK- it started out just like Tuesday and Wednesday but, instead of using the Lincoln, I figured I'd have better mobility on the Cow." His 1100cc Kawasaki motorcycle can go from Zero to a hundred in less than seven seconds. Just mentioning his baby, the Cow, brought a smile to his face and calmed him somewhat.

"I parked the bike up the hill a ways from their drive, but where I could still see it. I played around like I had engine trouble. After an hour of this I realized I hadn't picked the perfect surveillance spot. I was in direct line of sight from a neighboring house."

He shook his head from side to side as though denying it and went on, "Well, I started getting the hairy eyeball from the neighbor's gardener. You know what I mean: a big black guy on a cycle in that area. These aren't quite the enlightened times that some people would lead you to believe."

Nick was starting to relax, so I took this chance to sip at my coffee and nod encouragement for his narrative.

"Maybe I could've disguised myself as Nels, the Nordic Pool boy." He laughed and then said, "Naw, I couldn't live with any disguise that had the word, 'boy,' in it."

I got a mental picture of Nick in a blonde wig, wraparound sun glasses, and a powder blue Speedo. The image caused a snorting giggle to erupt from me. That earned me a glare and he said, "Before the locals were called to check on me, she came out of the driveway. On a bicycle, for crying out loud! Not that she didn't look kinda cute, mind you."

He followed with a technical description of exactly how much damage can happen to the mechanical innards of a high-powered super bike forced to follow a woman on a bicycle down a meandering country lane.

When I asked for his report, I didn't mean minute-by-minute. I guess he just needed to get every detail of this disaster off his chest, so I continued to humor him. Besides, the way he told it was entertaining.

"Anywhichway, she eventually got downhill to Aspinwall and along Freeport Road in the direction of Blawnox."

"The only way I could keep her in sight was to pass her, ride all around the block until I was behind her again. Then wait until she was nearly out of sight and then do it again."

I thought that, just maybe, his use of the Kawasaki on that particular day wasn't such a good idea. I said as much.

"Right," he agreed, "Even if she wasn't paying attention, I was starting to get noticed by people on the sidewalk just by circling the area so much."

I toyed with my latest gizmo that was lying on the desk. It was a nifty little digital recorder about twice the size of a pack of matches.

Nick was still talking, "She eventually pedaled her way to the Bitter Bay Sailing Club and Marina. I gave her a little lead then rolled into the marina and parked by the office. I was the object of at least a dozen less than friendly stares from a bunch of rich, I *mean rich white* folk. After all, I obviously wasn't a famous professional athlete, so I couldn't be one of their mascots.

"I just knew that one of them was about to tell me that all the maintenance and restaurant jobs were filled when I saw her get on a small express cruiser and motor away onto the river to god knows where."

I set aside my little toy, tented my fingers and waited for him to continue. What little calmness had settled on him was evaporating.

He continued, starting again to become agitated, "This woman sure made me feel dumb. I rode right out of there to the Avis office in Aspinwall where I rented the most invisible little compact on the lot. I left the Cow there, telling the rental clerk that I'd pick it up when I dropped the car off."

He finished his root beer and got up as though to get a refill. Instead, he placed his glass in the sink and resumed pacing the office as he said, "I didn't even have to think about it, right? I *knew* how the day was going to turn out. So I got a bag of burgers, a six pack of Pepsi and settled in near the Locke residence for the long haul. Just like clockwork, a little after six Wally Locke came down the road at the wheel of his Caddy. With the elusive towheaded Mrs. Locke riding shotgun."

He stopped in front of the book case to the right of my desk, staring unseeingly at the titles on the spines. I though he was done talking. So far we had spent fifteen hundred of our client's dollars with nothing to show for it other than a couple of turnpike receipts, a bill for a rental car and Nick's upset stomach.

I tried to ease his mind by saying. "You now, there's nothing you could've done. Sometimes weird things just happen."

I was sounding like a broken record.

"PT," he said, "You sound like a broken record."

In this business, we like to say that there are no coincidences, only things made to look like them.

"Nick, what do you think of this thought: maybe you were set up by the Lockes, either Mr. or Mrs. or both? These so-called losses of surveillances on your part sound too pat to be anything other than engineered. It sounds to me like she knew that you would be tailing her and she planned everything in advance to lose you in such a way that you wouldn't be able to resume the tail."

He smiled and said, "You mean I was set up?"

It isn't often that I have ever seen someone happy to have been set up, but there it was. It left him off the hook and restored his not inconsiderable professional pride.

"Whatever happened, it's over now," I said, "I'll run it by Will and get his opinion. But I think it was a prearranged job from the outset."

Humming to himself, he left my office after having told me to expect a detailed surveillance report in a couple of days.

"That rhymes with, 'witch,' won't lose me again," he happily opined.

I went into Will's lair and plopped myself down in my most favorite of the leather chairs that formed a semi-circle in front of his gargantuan desk. He was involved in some sort of intricate manipulation with a small gray plastic box on his blotter.

He turned it first one way, then another, all the while tugging at and pushing on various projections on the box. He then held it in the palm of his large brown left hand and poked it all over with his right index finger.

After a few moments, he sensed my presence and looked up. Face lined with consternation, he tossed the little box to me. It was quickly followed by a nine-volt battery and a request, "PT, can you get this damned thing open? The battery's dead and I can't open the garage door at the condo."

The little gray box bore the logo of a national manufacturer of garage doors. I took it in my left hand, slid the name plate aside and replaced the defective battery, and sent it back his way. He snapped the tossed gizmo out of the air.

"Thanks, PT".

Doing all these little impossible tasks has become a way of life for me. It's one of the reasons that I'm a kind of partner now, instead of the flunky he'd thought he was hiring.

"Will, we've got a problem with the Locke surveillance job. Nick can't keep track of her." That's like saying that Vanna White doesn't know the alphabet.

"What do you mean? Nick never loses track of a subject."

I related my phone conversation, omitting Nick's attempt at redemption through debauchery.

The whole time I was talking, Will was doodling on a large sketchpad on the right side of his desk. This habit of his is really disconcerting. He spends the time I'm patiently explaining some complicated, convoluted occurrence by carefully making little cartoons all over the sheet, wrinkling his forehead in concentration. He even erases and redraws parts that don't suit him. You get the definite impression that he wishes you would shut up and go away.

You'd be wrong. That's just his way of concentrating on what you are saying. When he's really ignoring you he'll stare straight at you with an interested expression that actually means he wishes you would go away.

When I had finished, Will drew a couple of curlicues across the bottom of a drawing of a man standing next to a fire hydrant yelling something to a dog. "Now I'll just have to caption it and it'll be ready to send in." I forgot to mention that these little cartoons Will doodles while he's concentrating wind up on the pages of quite a few national magazines.

I wound up by giving Will my opinion that the Locke woman had advance knowledge of the tail and was having fun setting Nick up.

"I'll call Locke and feel him out. I won't tell him that our man can't keep surveillance on his wife, but it sounds like something isn't quite kosher."

I went back to my office by way of Pamula's desk and asked her if she wanted anything from Scotty's for lunch. It looked like one of those days when we would be going to eat at our desks. She asked me to order her one of Scotty's famous jumbo fish sandwiches with a side order of fries and slaw.

I phoned in our order and poured myself another mug of coffee.

"Detective Shallenberger to see you, PT."

# CHAPTER 10 – A CAGE IS RATTLED

"What can I do for you, Detective Second Grade Shallenberger, or should I just call you sir?" His sartorial splendor was hurting my eyes. Somehow he managed to mix a florescent green color shirt with a yellow and brown plaid jacket set off by robin's egg blue trousers in such a way as to make the whole ensemble seem to be moving, even when he was still.

"Knock it off, O'Connor. It looks like we got off on the wrong foot from the first time we laid eyes on each other. If we can't be friends, let's try to be civil, at least."

I could barely hear what he was saying, what with all the warning bells and sirens going off inside my head. This guy was up to something.

"OK, Shallenberger." Better play it close.

Shallenberger and his partner made themselves comfortable in my office, sitting in a couple of my grandmotherly overstuffed chairs. Todd's colorless camouflage blended perfectly into the background fabric of the chair he chose.

"It looks like you're playing with some high-powered low-lifes. Aren't you afraid you might be getting out of your league?" Shallenberger seemed mighty concerned with my welfare.

"Jeez, I dunno detective. I have been looking over my shoulder a bit since someone tried to kill me. I mean shotguns and all. I don't remember the shotgun. If I did, I probably would've dirtied myself. I sure hope you guys straighten this out before something else happens."

I was laying it on thick, maybe too thick. Maybe this pair wouldn't go for it.

But they did. Shallenberger informed me of the Mosticello-Saint Martin connection. He also informed me that Saint Martin had out-of-town connections that could be dangerous to my health.

Todd contributed to the conversation by saying, "A paraffin test on McClymonds' hands showed that he had recently fired a weapon of some type. So, in all probability, it was McClymonds that took the pot shot at you."

I knew otherwise, but kept my mouth shut about that as I asked, "Does that mean you've found the shotgun?"

I guess that, figuring that Todd had had his moment in the sun, Shallenberger waved his hand dismissively in the air and said, "Naw, it probably disappeared when his buddy made tracks."

I offered the pair a cooling drink, but they declined telling me that it was shaping up to be a busy day for them and that they had to be on their way.

Shallenberger concluded by warning me, "You know, O'Connor, the last person that I know of who fooled around with this group and lived wound up in the witness protection program. Maybe you'd better leave this investigation to the police so's you don't get hurt, or worse."

I heartily thanked the pair of detectives for the information as well as for the investigation they were conducting. I also thanked them for handling something like this that was beyond my meager talent and capacity. I didn't tell them that I was going to stop working on the case.

It was getting on towards noon, so I popped over to Scotty's and picked up our order. I dropped Pamula's off at her desk, put mine in my office and was walking into Will's office to give him his. As I put my hand on the knob, I could hear Will's voice rising in a crescendo from a murmur to a bellow, "What the hell do you mean, my man must've been following her double? What double?"

Being familiar with Will's temper when aroused, I edged into his office, placed his order on his desk, and beat a hasty retreat to my office where I ate my lunch and watched the noon news.

A few minutes later I was summoned to his office where a calmer, gentler Will prevailed.

I plopped in my regular place and raised an eyebrow quizzically.

He finished the bite of sandwich that had been occupying him, washed it down with what appeared to be some of Pamula's fresh-squeezed lemonade, and said, "It seems as though Mr. Locke's personal assistant is just about a dead ringer for Vivien Locke, at least from any distance greater than twenty yards. Closer than that, and the twenty year difference in age becomes noticeable."

I rolled my eyes and looked at the Cutty Sark battling its way through

rough seas. I had an idea how the helmsman felt.

I said, "Nick was closer than twenty yards, and he doesn't make that kind of mistake."

Will replied, "On at least two of the days Wallace Locke says that Nick was following his assistant as she ran errands for him."

I came back with, "I wonder why he is lying about that. After all, it was he that asked us to shadow his wife."

Will replied, "Locke said that if Nick waited around long enough, he would have seen her drive the Caddy away. She usually keeps it overnight and drops in it at Locke's home in the morning when she gets her day's assignments. You can see how this mix-up could occur."

I responded that I could see how the mix-up *could* occur, but it seemed strange that it *would* occur, especially three days in a row.

Will acknowledged the adage that coincidences just don't happen in our line of work and directed me to find out as much as possible about Wallace *and* Vivien Locke.

Once again back in my office, I called Nick on his cell phone and told him to drop the tail for the time being. I needed him to garner as much background as possible on the Lockes. I said that he could call in as much help as he needed because I needed the information before the day was out. He said something to the effect that he does the difficult immediately and the impossible shortly thereafter. I didn't tell him that he stole his motto from the Seabees.

After all the movement and running around that had gone on all day, the sudden lull in activity made me feel antsy. So I figured, what better time to go rattle Danny the Dude's cage?

Not knowing what to expect, I unlocked my upper left hand drawer and extracted a couple chunks of metal.

The first was a relatively small frame .380 caliber semiautomatic seven-shot pistol. It went nicely into an ankle holster on my left leg. The second was a .357 magnum, double-shot derringer. It fit into a small pocket I have had sewn into all my trousers right behind my belt buckle.

Those silver and turquoise western style belt buckles I wear aren't really a fashion statement. Although Beth has from time to time mentioned that they make an obvious fashion impairment statement.

Suitably equipped, I was ready to face what may come my way. I carry a firearm only when I am going into a situation where I feel that my life may be in danger.

There are reasons for this, the most important of which is that carrying a firearm gives me a subconscious feeling of invincibility. This tends to affect my decision- making process in such a way that bravado replaces common sense.

I have talked with many other private investigators and off-duty police officers. The majority agree with me. When you unholster a firearm, there will be one of three outcomes, all bad.

First, there is the possibility that the gun will be taken from you and used on you. This is not good.

Second, you may shoot the wrong person, or an innocent bystander. This also is not good. Under the law you are responsible for each and every bullet you fire.

Third, you may shoot and kill the person you are aiming at. How can this be bad? That decision to fire that you made in a split second is going to be examined under a microscope at length by any number of law enforcement agencies. These include local police, county homicide investigators and the coroner's office. Each of these will question whether there was any other possible way for the situation to have been handled, *including running away*.

If any of these agencies decides that there was another way, you will be charged with something running the gamut from Violation of the Uniform Firearms Act up to, and including various degrees of homicide.

All of these things mean lawyers, which mean money.

Then, just when you think you are free and clear the federal government steps in with an investigation concerning the possible violation of the victim's civil or human rights. This costs more money.

Finally, when all the various departments of government have decided that you were justified in the shooting, relatives of the criminal you shot file a wrongful death suit against you in civil court.

So, you see, even if you are right, three or four years of your life have been lived under the pall of suspicion, and you are now bankrupt.

As if all this weren't enough, you now have to live the rest of your life knowing that you have extinguished the life of another human being. To paraphrase a famous fictional detective, "That's the stuff that nightmares are made of."

Even taking all this into consideration, the consensus among police officers and private investigators is that we would rather be judged by twelve than carried by six.

With this happy thought foremost, I took a company car and headed for Danny Saint Martin's digs in the Morningside section of the city. The Regis J. McKinley Reading and Benevolent Society was located in the middle of a block of connected buildings on Liberty Avenue not far from West Penn Hospital. Both sides of the street are lined with parking meters that are occupied twenty-four hours a day. I have never seen a car with a Pennsylvania license plate have any unexpired time on the meter. Likewise, the larger the car, the less likelihood that it would be decorated with a parking ticket. Even meter maids owe their jobs to someone.

The closest I was able to park to the club was three blocks away. It's amazing how quickly skin can chafe under an ankle holster, particularly when the combination of heat and humidity send the heat index through the roof.

The club is on the second floor of the building housing Rinky and pre-mortem Dinky's favorite restaurant and meeting place. The first floor exterior is a storefront with huge plate glass windows bisected by the recessed entry door. As I entered, I observed that the glass door and windows have been made of unusually thick glass. My, someone was paranoid.

Entering the establishment got me assaulted by modern American pizza shop ersatz Italian décor. The walls had framed, faded, and dusty travel posters that extolled the virtues of Roma, Napoli, and Firenza. Notices for local church bingos and Italian Day at Kennywood Park flanked pseudo marble statues that were supposed to evoke the atmosphere of Etruscan gardens. Six square tables covered in red gingham surrounded with whip back chairs were equipped with salt, pepper, red pepper, and Parmesan dispensers to complete the effect.

I walked to the rear of the eatery and noticed four swivel stools bolted to the floor in front of the counter that extended across the back of the room. On one of those stools, next to the huge ornate brass cash register, perched a waitress of indeterminate age and ethnicity. She had a proprietary air about the tables as though they were the income-generating machines she wished they were.

Noises emanating from the room behind the counter indicated that a kitchen was located back there. That, and the pervasive aroma of cheese, sausage, oregano and tomato completed the effect.

Immediately to her right was a well-worn door leading, in all probability, to the nonpublic areas of the club. Walking purposefully toward that door, I had my progress arrested by that waitress.

She blew a tendril of from-the-bottle blonde hair up and away from where it had encroached over her left eye and said, "Hon, that's the door to the club. Yinz can't go in there lessen yer a member. An' yinz don't look like no member to me."

I gave her what I calculated was my most winsome smile and replied, "Hello. I was told that I might meet Danny Saint Martin here. My name is PT O'Connor."

She walked around to the rear of the cash register and reached under the counter. A raucous buzz emanated from the door, unlocking its electric lock.

"Yinz just don't look the type... "

The door opened to reveal a steep, narrow wooden-treaded stairway with cracked peeling walls the color of ocher despair. Only one person at a time could fit on these stairs, precluding a rush on the door at the top.

There was no landing at the top, only the solid wooden door with the peep hole.

The door opened as I raised my hand to knock. Two disgustingly healthy-looking gym rats were on either side of the door opening.

"Yinz come to see Danny?" one of the behemoths assaulted my nun-installed grammatically correct sense of communication for the umpteenth time that day.

I nodded. They stepped aside letting me through the door. Once the door closed and locked behind me, one gentleman preceded me. The other followed.

The second floor bore absolutely no resemblance whatsoever to the ground floor. Here, everything was subdued: mahogany, leather, damask and velvet. Quiet tinkling of crystal, silverware and china could be heard coming from the screened-off private alcoves in the dining room. An unobtrusive wait staff could be felt rather than seen carrying out their duties.

We passed by the dining room and into a splendidly appointed lounge. Once again a number of screened-off alcoves provided privacy for those who wished it. The luxurious mahogany décor seamlessly evolved into a walnut and brass one evocative of an old seafarer's home. I knew that Will would heartily approve of the décor. I also knew that Danny the Dude had nothing to do with its selection. A discreet bartender was polishing glasses behind the ten-seat bar while a few habitués occupied a third of the captain's chairs cum bar stools.

The "doormen" showed me the way to one of the alcoves in the corner farthest from the entrance, but with a clear view of it. The man I had come to see sat at an octagonal table encircled by comfortable looking chairs with the smell of real leather. He pointed at one. I sat. The health club refugees silently faded from sight, but I am sure that they were both available to Mr. Saint Martin in an instant should the need arise.

Up close and personal, Danny exuded a forced charisma much like a barker for a strip joint. He just seemed ever so slightly out of sync with his surroundings like a charcoal grey suit in a line of pall bearers all wearing black. His curly black hair was too glossy, his teeth too white, fingernails too manicured. His tie was just a touch too scarlet. His tailored suit fit uncomfortably perfect.

He held up a cocktail glass in a mock toast, saying, "What can I do for you, Mr. O'Connor? What would you like to drink?"

"A glass of tonic with a twist of lime would serve to clear the dust from my throat."

One appeared in front of me, on a cocktail napkin, as if by magic. A quick turn of my head caught a glimpse of movement as the unobtrusive bartender returned to his post.

"Mr. Saint Martin, it's not what you can do for me so much as it is what I can do for you. I can save you endless trouble and aggravation."

His counterfeit smile began to weaken at the corners of his mouth.

"I have a fair idea of why you want the South Side Wrecking Company's plant and property. I also have a fair idea how badly you want it. If you are willing to cut your losses right now and drop it, we are willing to let bygones be bygones. By the way, extortion notes are a bit...childish, shall we say?"

His sham of a smile was no longer evident. His clenched jaw now matched the brittle hardness of his eyes.

"However, if you decide to continue on your present course of action, and anything untoward should happen to Mr. Clarence Darrow Reynolds, I will destroy you."

I took a sip of my tonic water and enjoyed watching Danny the Dude's countenance change chameleon-like, from tanning bed tan to red to pale. I heard the sound of breaking glass and saw blood trickling from his clenched left fist. He was, for the moment, speechless.

"Should you decide to behave as a proper businessman and tender a reasonable offer, it will be considered. However, any more visits from your heavy-handed thugs will result in their apprehension, conviction and incarceration. Any more attempts on my life will be met with an overwhelming response."

The very air in the lounge was vibrating with Danny's captured rage seeking an outlet.

"Please be reasonable and save us all a lot of unprofitable trouble."

As one final jibe to provoke him, I said, "On a more personal note: if I get any more of those annoying telephone calls I am going to personally insert that tool of communication against the normal flow of one of the major intestinal tracts of your body."

With that, I finished my drink, deliberately set the glass on its coaster and casually took my leave, once again walking through the lounge area and the dining area en route to the stairway door. I left Danny sputtering.

During the entire stroll to the exit, I had a tight spot between my shoulder blades, expecting some sort of attack. Nothing happened. I opened the door and entered the stairwell. As the door closed behind me I heard an anguished scream, "I'll kill the bastard."

I was back at the office before four and immediately briefed Will on what had transpired.

"Didn't I ask you not to make a scene?" Will inquired as though her were admonishing an eight year old.

"I'm sorry, Boss," I said insincerely.

"PT, take my advice and wear a vest until this thing is over."

I told him I'd consider it. I lied. Those things are too bulky, hot, and constrictive for my taste. Besides, they don't protect your head.

# CHAPTER 11 – CONNECTIONS

It was getting on toward evening, my private line rang. It was Nick.

"PT, this is costing a bit. I had to call in some outside help." I told him no problem, we needed to move on this. He proceeded to prove to me that the impossible only takes a few hours and asked where we could meet so he could fill me in.

I wasn't in the mood for sandwiches and a beer, so I suggested that we met at a restaurant on Murray Avenue in Squirrel Hill that was famous for the quality of their seafood. Since it was about halfway between us in distance, and he had a weakness for broiled lobster tail, he agreed.

Twenty minutes later found me entering the lounge area of the quietly busy restaurant. I scanned the walls to see if any of the family that operated this establishment had added to the collection of previously living behemoths of the deep festooning the walls. There were none that I considered worthy of comment. Harry, one of the owners, greeted me and told me that Nick was at the bar waiting for me. He was, with a single-malt scotch in front of him and a tall frosty glass of mint-garnished iced tea for me.

As I took the stool next to him, he spoke to my reflection in the back bar mirror. "I figured that you were going to go back to the office, so I didn't order you anything alcoholic."

I muttered my appreciation at his foresight and suggested that we get a table. Knowing the right people is an advantage. A healthy young lady acting as hostess led the way to a back corner table on the balcony overlooking the lounge. It was an ideal location for serious conversation with no worry about privacy. She gave each of us a billboard sized menu and departed with a smile.

When our waitress arrived, I set the menu aside and ordered the special of the day, Creole-style crayfish on a bed of wild rice with a side of mixed southern-style vegetables. I decided to start with a simple tossed salad.

Nick, on the other hands, ordered his standard fare for this place: a two-pound broiled lobster with drawn butter, baked potato and side dishes. As an afterthought he ordered a 12 ounce New York Strip, "Rare, so it melts in my mouth," as a chaser.

While we waited for our salads, he sipped from his scotch and started his report.

"Howard Locke is a local boy. He even graduated from Taylor Alderdice High School just around the block from here. He was a nerd. Three out of his four years he got a perfect attendance award and he graduated with high honors twenty four years ago."

I looked up at him from buttering my warm dinner roll and commented, "Wow- I guess there really is a, 'permanent record,' somewhere."

Nick ignored my attempt at levity and continued, "He got both a BS in metallurgy and a BA in business administration from the University of Pittsburgh a scant five years later. At that point he entered the employ of Universal Steel as a junior, junior executive. Three years later, with an MBA from Duquesne University acquired at night school in hand, he hopped on the fast track becoming a department head in less than ten years. That's when he hooked up with Vivien."

At this point the arrival of our salads interrupted his report and we dug in with gusto, leaving not so much as a shred of lettuce on our plates.

We shoved the plates to one side, awaiting our entrees. Nick picked a piece of greenery from between his bicuspids with his little fingernail, cleansed his palate with another swallow of scotch and continued, "That brings us to our darling, little Vivien Locke, previously known as Vivvy Kurhansky.

"She hails from Morningside, just a hop, skip and a jump from Lawrenceville. She grew up in a working stiff family where a Saturday glass of beer and a Kielbasi sandwich was more appreciated than a wine cooler and sushi."

"And yet she wound up in Fox Chapel," I commented, "Is this a great country, or what?"

"I'll get to that," he said. "She was a product of Saint Raphael's grade school and Cathedral high school. She followed that with a stint at a local business school where she learned office skills. Then she got a job at Universal Steel where she learned office politics."

Our waitress drifted by, refreshed our drinks and asked if everything was to our liking. We assured her that it was and continued our conversation.

"Guess who took our little sweetie to her senior prom?" Nick asked.

I admitted that I didn't have that knowledge and he replied, "Danny Saint Martin, that's who. In those days he was known as Dante Santa Marianna."

I knew about the name change, but I didn't want to interrupt, so I just managed to put a surprised look on my face and motioned for him to continue.

"After she was at Universal Steel for a while, she identified Wallace Locke as singled out for promotion and ascertained that she could control him with blonde hair, blue eyes and a nice butt. Before the poor s.o.b. knew what was happening to him, he had a wife. One with expensive tastes."

Our entrees arrived. We set to work demolishing them and in a short while, our table looked like a crustacean's nightmare. Limbs, claws and bits of exoskeleton heaped in little piles suggesting a maritime massacre.

Sooner than we would have liked we were drinking our after dinner coffee and sampling some of the best Key Lime Pie ever made outside of the Florida Keys.

Nick wiped his mouth and started in again, wanting to finish his report.

"Well, in no time at all, Mr. Wallace Locke found himself up to his nondescript neck in debt for furniture, real estate, club memberships, clothing and cars, all to keep her happy. Before marriage, he lived modestly in a courtyard apartment in Hampton Township, drove a compact sedan and put most of his income into savings and a stock portfolio. After Vivien got her hooks into him, that all changed.

"While he wasn't living beyond his means, he no longer had much in the way of a rainy-day plan. This was all because his little lady was now living in Fox Chapel in the manner to which she wanted to become accustomed."

By the time we had finished our desserts and coffees I learned that Vivien had two older brothers and two older sisters. Her oldest brother Stanley, (Stush to his friends), was a heavy equipment operator and a commercial truck driver. He drove a huge cement mixing truck for R. R. Smith. Small world.

Her other brother, Ronnie, used to work in the office at the PPG Plant in Creighton, but got layed off. Stush got him a job in the maintenance office at the trucks' garage. Must've been one hell of a prom night.

Nick finished up by saying, "Both of her sisters are married: Trish to a computer geek and Holly to a service station owner. Each has a squalor of children and looks ten years older than their birth certificates say they are."

I thanked Nick and agreed with him, "You do perform the impossible in a short period of time."

He replied, "You don't get off that easily," and slid the check across the table to me.

You know what? He wasn't in the least insulted that I paid the check with a company card.

Half an hour later found me back at the office, once again discussing the way all our current ventures meshed.

"I have that feeling that we have all the pieces. Now we just needed to assemble the puzzle in a way that makes sense," I proclaimed.

Will felt the same way. He slid the painting of the Cutty Sark aside revealing a black board and said, "PT, let's go over what we have so far on these cases and see if we can't figure out how they are connected."

First he drew a small circle in the bottom middle of the blackboard and labeled it, "Unk's Scrap Yard."

Next he drew a circle in the upper right corner and labeled it, "Danny Saint Martin."

"Uncle Clarence's scrap yard is at the bottom of everything," Will observed, "Why would anyone want 90 acres of nearly worthless industrial land?"

It was my turn. I drew a circle in the upper left corner and labeled it, "Vivien Locke." A line between her name and Danny's indicated that they had a relationship. Just below that line, I drew another circle and labeled it, "R. R. Smith." One line led from the circle to Danny's circle and one led to Vivien's circle indicating that they both had a personal interest in the company.

More circles were drawn. One below Danny's for Rinky and Dinky connected both to Danny's and the Scrap Yard's circle.

One below R. R. Smith's for Gummert Construction connected to Danny on one side and Vivien on the other side.

Wallace Locke had his circle below Vivien's. He connected with Universal Steel and with Vivien. Vivien also connected with Universal Steel. Universal Steel and Gummert Construction were connected as well.

All roads lead to Vivien. Two of her brothers worked for R.R. Smith, supposedly owned by Danny Saint Martin's mother. One of her brothers-in-law, who used to work in information technology in the city planning commission office, now worked for Gummert Construction, which just ordered massive amounts of construction equipment. Her husband, VP of

Distribution at Universal Steel, just upped production.

Danny seemed remarkably insulated on the drawing. In actuality, his connections were stronger than they appeared.

The diagram cleared things in Will's mind. He said, "On one side it looks like a gearing-up of major site prep and construction companies is taking place."

"And over here," He pointed to the opposite side of the diagram. "Danny Saint Martin is putting the squeeze on Unk for his property."

"Yeah, "I interjected, "But he's doing it through his intermediaries."

"Someone is trying to keep the connection between the build-up of construction capability and the acquisition of Unk's land less than obvious."

"Will," I said, bringing up the calculator program on his computer, "Let's see just how much is involved in cleaning up Unk's property."

Toxic substances of every imaginable type were on this land for so long that the clean-up would cost a fortune. The top two feet of soil will probably have to be replaced with clay, and then covered with topsoil.

Nearly two-thirds of a million cubic yards of material would have to be moved, just to make the land usable. Gummert Construction has just ordered all the earth moving equipment it could afford.

Will looked at the bottom line on the monitor, shook his head and commented, "As it stands right now, there is nobody involved in this scheme with a large enough bank account. Either we're looking at it from the wrong angle, or there's someone else involved that we are unaware of."

What would make the land so valuable as to justify this kind of expense? For one, off-track-betting. But slot machines were needed to make it viable. It looked like slot machines were going to be limited to the racetracks themselves. At $50 million per, slot machine licenses were only going to those people with really deep pockets.

Upscale housing? Not at a per-acre cost exceeding $1 million dollars before construction.

I mentioned to Will, "How about a really, really big ice arena with on-site parking, super-expensive condos, and a mall and entertainment complex?"

"You know, PT, that's an idea that just might have legs. Let's crunch some numbers."

"The current arena, including parking, is only a few acres."

"What figure was City Hall bandying about as a replacement cost for the Mellon arena?"

"I think it was in the neighborhood of $60 to $80 million."

I wet a paper towel at Will's sink and wiped all traces of our doodling from the chalkboard.

"Nice neighborhood. Compared to the cost of a slot license, it's low rent. You know, I think we're barking up the wrong tree with this one. I don't think an ice arena is the answer. Somehow or another, that slot machine license just has to figure in this."

He slid the painting back into place saying, "Well, let's just put it to bed for now. It's been a long day."

He concluded reminding me about the morrow's barbecue. He gave me directions and told me it would get under way around four in the afternoon.

I finished up a few remaining chores, closed up the office and went home. For some reason or another, I was still wearing the derringer.

There were two messages on my machine. For a change neither threatened my life. One was from Beth and the other I recognized as a cryptic message from Exie.

My appetite was still pleasantly sated from my earlier repast with Nick, so I just poured myself a tall cold glass of milk. Now, what's a glass of milk without a chocolate chip cookie? I put one on a napkin, carried it and the milk into the living room, and called Beth. She answered on the third ring.

"Hello."

"Hi hon, it's me. What's up?"

"PT, I've been thinking about what we discussed the other night."

I washed down a bite with a swallow of milk and replied, "And?"

"Here goes: the way it looks is that neither Saint Martin nor the Independents are making threats on your life. These guys just aren't the kind to make meaningless threats."

Great. Now I had someone else to worry about. With my mouth full of milk I managed to mumble, "How so?"

"These guys might give you one warning and that's it. For one thing, they just haven't got the imagination for a drawn-out terror campaign."

I wiped away the milk that had dribbled down my chin. After she had finished her thoughts, I filled her in on what Will and I had been discussing.

She digested this latest information, and then resumed, "It looks as though someone is planning a really major construction job on the site of the scrap yard. It also sounds like Vivien Locke is at the center of it all. If you find out where she is going when Nick loses her, I'll bet you can figure this thing out.

"As a matter of fact, I think this whole thing with Wallace Locke having suspicions about his wife's infidelity is a set up."

We finished our conversation and I hung up looking forward to seeing her the next day.

I figured out Exie's coded message to mean he wanted me to call him at his club.

Prepaid throw away cell phones are difficult to tap. That's why I've always kept a couple on hand. This seemed as good a time as any to use one.

I called him at the pay phone number of his club. It took a few tries, probably due to the number of errant husbands being paged by less than amorous wives who were left home staring at a cold Friday night dinner.

"O'Reilly here."

"Exie, it's PT. I'm using a safe phone."

"Good. I wanted to let you know: The bullet in McClymonds' head didn't come from the gun found with him. I came from one used in a homicide years ago."

I whistled soundlessly through my lips.

"That particular gun was one of a batch no longer needed for evidence. It was taken to a steel company and melted down to keep it off the streets. You know how the department does that from time to time as a publicity stunt. It makes Joe Citizen think we're actually doing something to keep the streets safe."

Something made me feel that this wasn't the real news. I asked, "What else?"

"Guess who signed for the batch of guns to be destroyed? Shallenberger and Todd, that's who."

This was a bombshell alright. I was just too tired to completely digest it at midnight.

Exie wasn't finished, "Look guy, I'm afraid I can't help you much more with this. If I keep nosing around, I'm sure to send up a few red flags to people that I would not want to notice me."

I assured him that he had done way more than anyone could expect and thanked him for his help. I told him to make sure that his tracks were covered and to steer clear of things for a while.

I guess it was the milk. I somehow managed to sleep like a baby.

# CHAPTER 12 – A GARDEN PARTY

Saturday morning. I was up and about before seven. A nice five-mile run through the early morning mist along the wet streets is just what it took to energize me. It was no longer night and not quite morning. The slight chill in the air held a promise of afternoon warmth. Ideal running weather.

Once I got into the rhythm of the run and my heart rate got up into the beneficial range, the muted slap-slap of my running shoes, the haloed streetlights and the deserted Saturday morning streets allowed my mind to drift over the events of the week without conscious effort on my part.

It's hard to describe the zone. Even while I'm paying close attention to my surroundings, my mind is fully concentrating elsewhere. Five miles of this concentration gave me a couple of ideas on how to unravel at least part of this case. Still I could not fit the puzzle together. A number of pieces were still missing.

After an exhilarating run, I returned home, got in the car and went to Jim's Gym for another workout. A couple of the faces in the gym seemed a bit too familiar to me, as though I'd seen them in another context.

By ten in the morning I was back home showered and totally refreshed.

I gave the truncated Saturday Edition of the paper a perfunctory glance: nothing of interest there.

Beth showed-up with the Blue Snake (That's what she named her Cobra Roadster) and we went out for lunch and a ride in the country with the top down before arriving at the party around 4:20.

The Squirrel Hill-Shadyside-Point Breeze areas of the City form a triangle and complement one another. Formerly where the high-society movers and shakers of the industrial age with names like Mellon, Carnegie, Heinz and Westinghouse would go to avoid rubbing elbows with the sweaty working class, they are today's status addresses of the literati, thespian, legal and medical professions of the city.

There is even a well-respected private college hidden in this pastoral escape from the city's former industrial maelstrom. Many of the mansions have been turned into apartments and lofts for students, educators, artists and others who can both afford the rent and appreciate the surroundings.

The address on Hyacinth Lane was not one of these. A small brass plaque at the end of the shaded curving driveway merely stated, "610 – Howard." Following the drive brought us to the front of a solidly built granite mansion in the style of the German stonemasons who designed and constructed most of these monuments to manufacturers.

Somehow, Uncle Clarence's daughter managed to turn that imposing edifice into a welcoming one. She did this with strategically planted bright flowers on an open expanse of lawn while breaking up the harshness of the building's original lines with bright pennants and draperies.

We parked at the front alongside a Nissan, a Caddy, and a low-slung purple, pink and green S-10 pickup with darkly tinted windows. The Caddy bore no signs of its previous encounter with spray-painted window tinting. Will's personal car, a jet-black Chevy Impala, was at the far end of the line.

Muted strains of indeterminable music wafted their way from the rear of the house.

A bundle of energy dressed in the wildly contrasting yet harmonious colors of the Caribbean swept toward us through a brick archway from the direction of the music. As this explosion of energy and color approached us, I could see that it consisted of an immensely attractive, short buxom woman of caramel color who was all smiles and exuded joyfulness.

She encompassed us both in a hug that drew us into her aura of goodwill while gushing, "You must be the young people Uncle Clarence has told us so much about- I don't mean that he has told us anything negative- It was all good things that he said- Of course Uncle Clarence never says anything bad about anybody- But you know that, if you know him- And Will and his lovely wife Pamula are here as well- And you can meet my daughters and their beaus- I do hope you like island food- I mean food from the islands, not Hawaii- the Caribbean Islands- like Jamaica, Haiti and the Virgin Islands- Not that the Hawaiian Islands have bad food, but-."

A tall muscular man with steel wool eyebrows, hair and mustache materialized at her side. With twinkling eyes and a welcome smile, he extended his hand, "Hello, I am Clarence Reynolds and you have already met my daughter Celeste Howard. Welcome, welcome. Will and Pamula have told me much about you. I am in your debt."

We walked around the house to the rear, where a large in-ground pool was located in a clearing surrounded by mountain laurel.

Will and Pamula were relaxing by the edge of the pool sipping something tropical. In the water were four young people cavorting and splashing.

Beth and I quickly changed in the poolside cabana and joined the others. I wore my usual wildly flowered swim trunks that have increased the sale of sunglasses at more than one swimming hole. Beth, on the other hand, wore a brief something-or-other that nobody would remember anyhow. All anyone would remember was an expanse of flawless skin accentuated here and there with equally flawlessly placed curves.

Celeste swept us up in her own personal whirlwind once again, "Kids-come over here. PT and Beth, I like you to meet my daughters, Jacquetta and Jeanetta."

Tall, slender, long-necked Nubian princesses wearing the briefest of bikinis somehow managed to exude innocence, charm and sexuality at once.

Jacquetta, slightly taller and the elder at 23 entwined her arm with a muscular young black man's and said, "This is my friend, Issac Bradley, maybe you've heard of him by his stage name, T-B-T-B Phly. He's a singer."

The young man in front of me wearing the dread locks immediately extended his dragon-tattooed arm, gave me a firm handshake and said, "Call me Issac." He pronounced it "Iss-Sack."

He had an easy-going smile that extended to his eyes. However, there was something lurking in those clear maple syrup eyes that made you want to avoid troubling him.

"Certainly. Call me PT."

"Jacquie's told me about what you've been doing for her, her family."

I mumbled something self-deprecating. All this gratitude was starting to bother me.

Celeste's other, equally beautiful daughter, shyly extended her hand and said, "Hi I'm Jeanetta. This is my friend, Dewayne. He's a reporter for The Sentinel."

Dewayne had that unhealthy appearance of one who spends too much of his life in places where both light and warmth are absent. He was somewhat tallish with spindly, too-long extremities, a sallow complexion, and coke-bottle glasses.

Alarms went off in my head. The Sentinel was a local black-oriented newspaper whose only reason for existence seemed to be to foment problems between the races.

He offered a handshake that went with his appearance and said, "Jeanetta flatters me. I write fillers, obits and fluff that no one else wants to do."

Behind his smile was something that exuded intensity without substance, like a strobe light in a smoke cloud.

I took his hand, "Glad to meet you, Dewayne."

I was unable to make a connection with either of the young men. Hip-hop music wasn't my forte and the plight of the downtrodden Black Man didn't seem quite applicable in these surroundings.

On the other hand, Uncle Clarence or, as he preferred to be called, "Unk," and I hit it right off. He, Will, and I conversed about a wide range of subjects unrelated to Unk's problems.

Meanwhile, Celeste, Pamula, and Beth were finding that they also had quite a few interests in common. In no time they were gabbing like long-lost friends.

After a sumptuous feast of lobster, steak and prawns grilled over charcoal to perfection by Unk, evening descended and we moved inside. Nightfall found everyone in the drawing room of the house enjoying a nightcap before leaving.

Jacquetta and Jeanetta and their boyfriends made their escape from us "old" folks and went out. After all it was Saturday night.

Jacquetta and Issac were bound for the Strip District and an evening of club hopping, while Jeanetta and Dewayne were on their way to a lecture about the history of slavery in America and its impact on modern culture.

We wound up seated at the kitchen table kibitzing over minted iced tea and citrus salad. Unk sat at one end of the table, Celeste at the other, Will and Pamula on one side and Beth and I on the other side.

After a time, Unk cleared his throat and said, "I hate to be one who throws a wet blanket over such a pleasant gathering, but there are a couple of serious things that need our attention."

Will said, "PT you have the floor. Bring us up-to-date."

I summarized what we had learned: Unk's scrap yard sits on some of the most valuable property in the state in spite of what it would cost to develop. People with political connections were already jockeying to make money from it. Certain unsavory characters wanted control of the property and were willing to go to great lengths to get it. One man is already dead who was involved in the plot.

"Unk, it seems as though all these people want your land before it becomes public knowledge what use is planned for it."

Some of this was news to Unk. All of it was news to Celeste, who exclaimed, "Dad! What do you mean by keeping all this from me? Don't you think I could handle it?"

Unk replied, "Come on honey. You know I wouldn't want to worry you with these things. You've got enough on your mind raising my two wonderful granddaughters. Now let's see what the young man has in mind."

Celeste retorted, "Stubborn old fool," but it was said with exasperated love.

I continued, "There are a couple of things we can do. I have a few connections with the area newspapers and can get some stories planted that will speculate about the suitability of your land for various uses, including the one we suspect. This will bring the whole thing into the open and may stop some of the behind-the-scenes manipulating to get your property on the cheap. On the other hand, it may have the effect of blowing-up the whole deal and leaving you right where you are now."

Nods of agreement were apparent around the table.

"Another tactic might be to deal with those entities who are interested in the property. If they realize that you know the value of your property, their methods of dealing with you will change. We have already started making steps in this direction."

I swiveled my head from one end of the table to the other and saw that both Unk and Celeste had quizzical expressions on their faces in response to my last statement.

"Finally, as a last resort, there are ways we can torpedo the whole shebang leaving everyone else out in the cold." I took a healthy draught from my iced tea and concluded, "It's up to you Unk."

It was Will's turn now. "Just remember, none of the options are without risk either financial or personal. Our first priority is the personal safety of you and your family."

Unk ruminated with a few sips of iced tea and then exhibited that inner strength that enabled him to go from a poor young black man with a decrepit pickup truck gathering junk and scrap to a wealthy businessman with a yearly payroll of over a million dollars.

"First, the safety and security of Celeste and the girls are of paramount importance. Nothing must happen to them.

"After that has been insured, I like the idea of taking the battle to our opponents and letting them be on the defensive. While they're ducking, they can't be throwing rocks."

He plucked a sliver of honeydew melon from his plate and ate it savoring every bit of it. When he was finished swallowing, he said, "Along these lines, Will, I would like you to check-up on these two young gentlemen who have garnered my granddaughters' affections."

Here Celeste took over and said, "This kind of talk will spoil my home made Pecan Pie. So, everyone hush up and enjoy."

That's what we did. We finished the evening with generous slices of Pecan Pie topped with scoops of Islay's vanilla ice cream.

# CHAPTER 13 - BEAUS

Monday morning. After an unusually relaxing weekend, feeling recharged and raring to go, I got to the office a bit early. As I was entering, a short balding man with an exquisite comb over and a suit already rumpled at 9:00AM was leaving.

I stopped at Pamula's desk and asked, "What's with the process server?"

She replied, "See Will."

I made a pot of my special blend and, mug in hand, went in to see Will.

"G'morning Boss."

"Morning, PT. Have a good weekend?"

I grunted in the affirmative and Will asked, "Well, what've you got on the burner for today?"

I mentioned those tasks that we discussed at the end of the night on Saturday, then sipped at my mug of coffee while Will outlined our campaign to settle things for Unk.

"Sounds good," he replied, "I've already got the ball rolling on some of it. I set up a 24 hour watch on Celeste's house with two people per shift. That way, if someone leaves the house, one of the operatives can remain while the other follows. Next, I set up a protective watch on Jacquetta and Jeanetta when they are away from the house."

He had a list and as he mentioned each item, he ticked it off.

"Then, I put a 24 hour uniformed guard at Unk's scrap yard, plus a 24 hour plainclothes guard."

"Sounds expensive."

"That it is. We are talking nearly 130 man hours per day. Not counting your time and my time. Conservatively, our expenses are running somewhat more than $2,500 a day. So, let's try to get this wrapped up ASAP."

I was reluctant to add to the load, but I had to tell Will about the history of the gun that killed McClymonds.

He said that he would have to think about that one and got out his doodling pad.

I made ready to leave, and Will looked up and said, "By the way we have a couple of problems."

I resettled in the chair, placed my mug down, and cocked an inquisitive eyebrow.

Will went on, "The gentleman who left as you arrived just served papers on us. An attorney acting on behalf of Mrs. Locke is filing suit for invasion of privacy and harassment, among other things."

I mentally tallied one for myself in the judge of character column. I dismissed the law suit, "That's why we have lawyers on retainer. What's the other problem?"

"The other problem, as you so glibly put it is that the attorney's quarterly retainer fee has not been paid and neither has the liability insurance premium. Neither has most of last month's bills. Do you have any thought about these things?"

It slowly dawned on me. Bundles of envelopes to be mailed given to me by Pamula on my way out to check on Rinky and Dinky. I put them in the glove compartment. What is left of the car is in the police impoundment lot with those envelopes still in it. It seemed like a lifetime ago.

"Uh Will. I'm sorry. I don't know what to say. I forgot all about them."

He dismissed me with a wave and said that Pamula would be able to handle most of the problem.

I hoped that a bouquet of flowers would express my contrition and thanks.

I returned to my office and got started on the background checks.

Armed with names and addresses, I was able to get birth dates and driver's license numbers. Cross referencing  those, I was able to get social security numbers. From this I found an avalanche of information about both men.

Issac Bradley was twenty-nine years old and had come from what is colloquially called the hood. The oldest son of a single parent, a father, he had two younger siblings, one brother and one sister.

He had the usual legal difficulties that a kid from the ghetto acquires: A couple of arrests for curfew violations, one for failure to disperse and one for disorderly conduct, all minor violations.

It wasn't Issac's high school grades that got him into the University of

Pittsburgh. His haunting, evocative poetry about ghetto life and unforgiving city streets won him a partial scholarship sponsored by one of the ultra affluent families of the city.

He supplemented that scholarship by working at a variety of menial jobs. These ranged from grass cutting, dish washing, and janitorial work to loading and unloading box cars. All these jobs had two things in common. They were physically demanding, while allowing his fertile and creative intellect to roam elsewhere.

After getting a Master of Fine Arts Degree from Pitt, he learned that there really wasn't much of a job market for aspiring poets, but a local trucking company was hiring. Loading trucks eight hours a day, five days a week, accounted for his impressive physique.

After a while at the trucking company, Issac discovered a way to derive income from his poetry. He adopted the moniker T-B-T-B-Phly, which translates as,"Too Baad Too Bee Phly," and entered the world of hip-hop music.

He was something of an anomaly in that he had gathered a fairly large local following for his gritty lyrics that spoke to his young audiences, both black and white, without resorting to profanity. Six years at the University of Pittsburgh gave him a vocabulary that allowed him to find the correct word without resorting to epithets. He was also known for his flamboyant manner of dress.

After four years of performing, he was able to quit his job at the trucking company and devote all his energies to his chosen calling: poetry.

Unknown to his fans, his poetry had been published in some of the country's most respected literary magazines.

Also unknown to his fans, he had been assiduously investing most of his income and was building a rather impressive portfolio, ranging from blue chip stocks and mutual funds to local construction companies.

All in all, Issac Bradley appeared to be a young man on track to becoming both a popular entertainer and a respected poet. That's about as much as I could learn without leaving my desk. I'd have to fill in the blanks about him by doing some old-fashioned legwork.

Using the same methods, I learned that Dewayne Collins was twenty-five years old and employed by the Sentinel as a sort of utility infielder. He covered everything from feature stories, breaking stories to obits, plus telephone answering, filing, and making pizza runs. It was a great way for someone to learn the newspaper business.

Dewayne is the youngest of eleven children born to a devout Christian couple. His father was a minister and his mother ran everything else about the small storefront evangelical church in the Hill District area of the city.

He graduated at the top of his class from one of the city schools. Having seen him Saturday night, I'll bet this earned him a few beatings from his peers. He was quite active in high school. He was editor of the school newspaper as well as the yearbook and a member of the debating team, the chess team, the honor society, and the school choral group.

Even though he was an excellent student, no scholarship came his way. In the city schools those are reserved for talented athletes, not scholars. Other than a flair for absorbing information in such a way as to be able to demonstrate an understanding of that information on test papers, Dewayne had no other talent and was relegated to being a member of the pack.

Dewayne worked his way through community college by doing shift work at fast-food restaurants, caddying at an upscale country club, and running errands for anyone who needed it.

Surprisingly, he also found time to get arrested a number of times at various rallies and demonstrations for disorderly conduct, failure to disperse and blocking traffic. This seemed to indicate that Dewayne was somewhat of an activist: nothing wrong with that.

That was about it for Mr. Collins without actually interviewing friends, acquaintances and relatives.

I wasn't sure whether Will would want a complete investigation or not. Sometimes it is hard to do so without alerting the subject that he was being investigated. Especially when you are in a hurry and apt to take short cuts.

My intercom light buzzed.

"PT, Detectives Shallenberger and Todd to see you."

I went to my office door, opened it, and called out to them, "Right this way, gentlemen."

Shallenberger helped himself to a cup of my coffee, added a bit of cream, took a sip and said, "O'Connor, this is some of the best coffee I've had in ages."

Todd, hovering almost unseen in the background also poured himself a cup.

I said I'd give him the recipe if he was interested.

"O'Connor, you live under a lucky star. We finally got the full coroner's report on the stiff in your trunk. Turned out that the gentleman had a .380 caliber semi-jacketed bullet in his head. Someone caved his head in with your tire iron after he was already dead camouflaging the entrance wound."

Yeah, like you don't know where the gun came from, I thought without giving voice to the thought.

"Any idea why someone would want to do that?" the detective asked.

I thought, why don't you ask yourself, but I said, "I don't know. Whoever did must know that it was just a delaying tactic at best. I'd look for someone who would benefit from a week out of the spotlight. Like maybe Danny Saint Martin? Of course, I didn't say that."

They finished their coffee and bid me adieu. And maybe, just maybe they were headed for the Reading Society.

I gave Will what I had on the boyfriends and he said that he would like a bit more background. He wanted to know what made them tick, what went on inside their heads, what motivated them.

I called Nick.

As soon as I finished with him, I got out a pad of paper and tried to organize my facts.

Beth called. "PT, I've been a little uneasy since Saturday. Something about Jeanetta's boyfriend, Dewayne, nagged at me."

"Uh-huh," I responded.

"You remember the time I spent with the DA's office as an assistant prosecutor? Well, I still have some contacts there and I decided to do a little checking on Mr. Collins."

I absently absentmindedly started drawing smiley faces on my notepaper while grunting an affirmative to her statement.

"Our Mr. Dewayne Collins is being investigated by certain people from the Department of Homeland Security. He used to be quite a militant supporter of black rights. Then, suddenly he faded from the scene. He still attends all the right rallies and demonstrations, but he is no longer one of the people on the front lines getting arrested with regularity."

I started tapping my desk top with the eraser end of the pencil. The smiley faces evolved into frowny faces with vampire fangs.

"He is no less political. His allegiance has just shifted from those who would work within the system to those who would overthrow the system. He has hooked-up with a group known as the Keepers of the Koran."

The frowny faces acquired pointy ears and slanted eyebrows.

Great, just great, I thought, now religion is going to enter the fray. Meanwhile, I was performing half of a drum roll with the pointed end of the pencil.

"This is a relatively small group, but it is a dangerous one. Its main reason for existence seems to be as a conduit along which money flows to other, better known terrorist groups. Members of this group take a vow of poverty and give everything they have to the group. They then expend all their energies in raising funds for the group.

"Some of their fund-raising techniques are suspected to be less than legal, and it is rumored that they have cells devoted to robbery, drug-dealing and kidnapping.

"P-T, I'm afraid that Jeanetta is a target for a kidnapping."

The pencil broke.

# CHAPTER 14 - UNLOCKE-ING DOORS

What in the hell else could go wrong on this sweltering July afternoon in Pittsburgh? Between lawsuits, insurance premiums, attorney retainers, and impending kidnapping, my world was just a bit unstable. What better way to stabilize my world than to shake up someone else's? A visit with Mrs. Locke was in order.

I pushed one side of the huge double front door open, remembered that I'd left something on my desk and turned to reenter the office. Just then a shower of splintering wood porcupined the back of my head. A split second earlier or two inches to the left and I'd be dancing with the Reaper instead of diving for the floor and rolling clear.

A tornado tore through the reception area leaving a scattering of tables, chairs and magazine racks in its wake. Will scrambled to my side, a huge 44 Magnum Auto Mag dwarfed in his massive right hand.

"PT. What th...You OK?"

After verifying that I wasn't discoloring the carpet with any body fluids, I replied in the affirmative, stayed clear of the door, and regained my feet.

"Uh, boss? I think that 'little job' for your uncle may be just a wee bit more complex than we have anticipated."

At the edge of my vision I could see Pamula returning the Ruger Mini-14 Carbine to its clips under her desk.

"Yes, I think I'll have to make a few calls."

My injuries consisted of a couple of superficial scratches that cleaned up quickly with a damp paper towel. I'd suffered worse while shaving.

We discussed notifying the police about the shooting, but decided to handle it ourselves. As things stood, it might've been the police doing the shooting.

Will handed me the slug that he dug from the door frame. "It's a .177

caliber pellet from one of those high-powered air guns."

That answered the question of why I hadn't heard a gunshot. I originally thought of a silencer. That wouldn't explain that mosquito whine I had heard *after* the shot.

Once my pulse rate achieved something approximating normal, I returned to my previous plan.

The trip from the office in Hazelwood to the Locke residence in Fox Chapel was about a half-hour by car but it was light years in wealth. Those who live in Fox Chapel limit their knowledge of how the less fortunate members of society exist to what they garner from their television sets.

According to the standards of the area, the Locke residence wasn't anything special. It was in that previously undeveloped section of the township where the nouveau riche was segregated from the old moneyed class. Set on a couple of acres, the house invisible from the road, it would have the usual accoutrements: in-ground pool, security-fenced and surveillance camera covered perimeter, gated drive, on-staff gardener, cook and maid.

Even so, those having had experience living somewhat below the economic stratum of the marina/country club/polo set will do anything to protect their existence in Fox Chapel. Anything.

I gained new appreciation for Nick's skills. I, for one, could not imagine how he set up a stakeout in this place, where the Neighborhood Crime Watch is a religion and paranoia is an avocation.

I gained entry by pushing the buzzer which was conveniently located next to the intercom and camera lens at driver's door height at the gate. When questioned as to my intentions, I merely said, "PT O'Connor to see the lady of the manor."

The gate slid smoothly and quietly out of the way and I drove through. My rear view mirror afforded me a view of it once again sliding smoothly back into place blocking the entrance. A small parking area at the main entrance circled a pool with a laughing dolphin puking water from his mouth. I chuckled to myself. How Hollywood.

The house itself, made of Ligonier granite, somewhat resembled a Swiss chalet with leaded-crystal windows and four-inch-thick oak doors. The front door swung open as I reached for the knocker. What appeared to be an old family retainer showed me in and escorted me to a comfortable study. Appearances are deceiving. The Lockes hadn't been here long enough to retain old anything.

He led the way to a small patio near the pool at the back of the house where I seated myself at a funny little white enameled patio chair beside a glass-topped umbrella table. Shortly, Mrs. Locke made her entrance. It wasn't what I expected of a Fox Chapel diva: she was wearing that ubiquitous uniform of the city's neighborhoods on house-cleaning day: blue jeans, flip-flops, a man's shirt tied at the waist and her hair restrained with a bandanna.

I rose to greet her. She briefly took my hand and inquired, "Mr. O'Connor, may I offer you some refreshments? Something to drink, perhaps?"

Shortly thereafter, a tall iced tea found its way to my hand by way of an unobtrusive maid and I sipped it appreciatively.

She seated herself across the table from me cradling a frosted mug of something looking like cola in her hands. She took a long drink from it and set it down on the glass tabletop where it immediately started making condensate puddles.

She pushed an errant blonde curl from her forehead, gave me her best ten-thousand dollar orthodontic smile and apologized for her appearance saying, "I've been rooting around in the attic for some antiques to donate to the annual Christmas Children's Relief Auction."

I could almost see the words ornately engraved in a dialog balloon over her head. I didn't mention that Christmas was the better part of four months away, nor that prevarication detracts from an otherwise beautiful set of porcelain crowns.

"Now then, Mr. O'Connor- what brings you to my home? My attorneys have advised me that there should be no communication between myself and anyone from your firm."

I was tempted to reach across and wipe a small smudge of soot from her left cheekbone. I resisted the urge. It made her look cute.

"Please just call me PT, Mrs. Locke. The reason for my visit is to ask you to call off the dogs. I think we can settle any difference between us without resorting to the court system."

"Mr. O'Connor," she said making a point of enunciating each syllable, "Invasion of my privacy is worth much, much more to me than a simple apology."

"I am so sorry, Mrs. Locke," I said with heavy emphasis on the so. "Did I give you the impression that I was here to apologize? If so, let me set you straight. There are certain things that are going to come out concerning the involvement of you and your husband with certain less than up-and-up municipal contracts. Not to mention the involvement of your extended family."

Her smile picked up that emotionless pasted-on countenance of a professional sensitivity suppressor.

I sipped at the lemon-flavored iced tea and continued, "I am paying you this visit in order to save you expense and embarrassment. I think that your involvement with certain contractors, city officials and less than ethical gentlemen from Morningside would encourage you to find adequate representation from criminal defense attorneys, not from those who specialize in tort law. And, what would the neighbors think?"

She wore her upper class socialite pasted-on smile until the word, "Neighbors." At that point her brow wrinkled, the smile became a grimace and she raised her chin showing every tendon in her neck ready to pop. And her eyes. Wow. Her eyes.

She didn't look cute anymore. She dropped her pseudo-British affectation and reverted to pure Pittsburghese.

"Yinz better get yer ass outta here right now! And it's yinzes that had better be watching yer ass from now on. I'm calling Danny right now."

I thanked her for the iced tea and admonished her not to expose the others involved with the Christmas Children's Relief Auction to such uncultured language ending with, "…it just wouldn't be ladylike, yinz know?"

She retorted with a stream of invective, concluding with, "Ya sunuvabitch, ya."

I think that I had heard the sound of shattering glass. I hoped the maid wouldn't cut herself cleaning it up.

I took my leave, my right temple pulsing, waiting for the blow from the rolling pin that had to have made its way to Fox Chapel from Morningside.

Someone was watching, because the driveway gate slid open to permit my egress as I approached it.

Once again I drove from one universe to another. This time it took only twenty minutes.

Even though a parking spot was available right in front of the Regis J. McKinley Reading Society, I still parked a half-block away. There was less than 500 miles on the odometer and I wanted to break in the new car before seeing it broken up.

The same waitress was near the cash register and she gave me a frown of recognition. Funny how I affect some people.

I went directly to the door leading to the upstairs club and gave her an inquiring look. She reached under the counter and I heard the buzz that unlocked the door.

This time, when I got to the top of the stairs I didn't stop. I shouldered my way by the gym rats, strode the length of the hallway, and entered Danny's little sanctum.

The door to the little bar area snicked shut behind me and I got that uncomfortable tingle right between my shoulder blades again.

There he sat quietly sipping from a glass of vegetable juice in all his sartorial splendor. Today he was dressed as a Mississippi River Boat gambler, all in creams and whites down to his walking cane topped with a chunk of crystal that looked like he stole it from my grandmother's bathroom door knob.

"Mr. Saint Martin, he just pushed past and we dint think that yinz wanted no gun play up here…"

"Of course, of course. Please be seated Mr. O'Connor. Fellows, Mr. O'Connor is welcome here at any time. Now, if you would please just leave us alone."

They backed out and I could imagine them scraping, bowing, and touching their forelocks to quit the presence of the emperor.

"Mr. O'Connor. You don't mind if I call you PT." It wasn't a question. "I'm afraid that we have gotten off to a bad start. Now, what can I do for you?"

I wanted some of whatever he had for breakfast. It did wonders for his disposition, maybe it'd do something for mine.

"Mr. Saint Martin. You don't mind if I call you Danny." It wasn't a question, either. "I think I can help you and I think you can help me. Someone's setting you up to take a fall. Right now I know how, I just don't know why, although I have a good idea who. I'll need your help to sort it out."

A glass of tonic with a wedge of lime quietly found its way to my elbow. Someone had a great memory.

Magnanimity flowed forth from his perfect smile. "I will try to help in any way I can, PT. You have no idea how much I would like to clear-up this little misunderstanding."

Yeah, right. I also knew how much he would like to bury me. "Thanks, Danny. Your assistance will be invaluable."

Then we sat together at his private booth to solve this conundrum and put our differences behind us. We discussed politics, ethnicity, neighborhood loyalties, cuckolded husbands, real estate values and childish harassment.

We seemed to have had a meeting of the minds on just about everything but the harassment. I didn't get the information I'd been hoping for on all those diverse subjects, but I did get a little. On that one, he categorically denied any knowledge whatsoever.

When I left, that damn tingly feeling between my shoulder blades just wouldn't go away. So much for *glasnost*.

# CHAPTER 15 - SKELETONS

I returned to the office at four and gathered my messages. The thought crossed my mind that Danny hadn't mentioned a visit by Shallenberger. I was disappointed. I just wasn't sure who I was disappointed with: Danny, for not mentioning the visit, or Shallenberger, for not making one.

Nick had called a couple of times, Beth had left a message for me to call her, Jacquie wanted me to call her back and there were a couple of messages I ignored.

I returned the most important call first and spoke with Beth. I assured her that we were using all the firm's assets to protect Jeanetta.

I called the number that Unk's granddaughter had left, but now *her* answering machine was on. It looked like we were destined to play a bit of phone tag.

Nick answered on the first ring when I called him. "PT, I'm glad you called back. Mr. Reynolds's granddaughters sure got a couple of characters for boy friends."

"OK, Nick, give me a run-down."

"First, this T-B-T-B Phly Issac Bradley character. He isn't anything like what he is supposed to be. While everyone else walks down the street next to the buildings so as to not draw the attention of the gang bangers, he swaggers right down the middle of the sidewalk all lit up like a neon sign saying, 'hit me, if you can.'"

"He doesn't even have any back-up with him. He is a one-man show." Nick said with incredulous respect.

I poured myself a Pepsi over ice as we conversed. It was too late in the day for coffee and July afternoons aren't conducive to hot drinks anyway.

He continued, "Now here's the best part. He's got respect from everyone in the hood. The gang bangers like him. The moms and pops like him. The kids like him. Hell, even the police like him."

I took a long draught, feeling all the cold little bubbles scour their way down my throat, clearing the dust from that pipe. I mumbled something that sounded encouraging to him.

"A little digging shows that he gives away a big chunk of his money to a rehab center for junkies and drunkies. It has something or other to do with his sister."

He didn't sound like a stereotypical rapper to me. Nick's voice indicated that he felt pretty much the same way.

"Besides his clothes, the only thing he spends money on is his ride, a real tricked-out little pickup truck."

I remembered the wildly colored little truck from the garden party at Celeste's and nodded agreement, even though Nick couldn't see me.

"The guy's got advanced degrees from Pitt, makes a decent living as a rapper, gives away part of his money to charity, is popular with everyone, still lives in the hood. I wouldn't be surprised to find out that he is a deacon in some church, too." Nick went on, "He sounds too good to be true. I'm going to keep checking."

"OK, Nick, most of what you got on Issac I already have. Keep digging and see what else turns up. What were you able to get on Jeanetta's guy?"

I started a fresh sheet in the note book.

Nick's tone and attitude both changed. His lack of respect for the younger sister's boyfriend was evident.

"Dewayne Collins is a sleaze. He's the kind of punk that'll tell you whatever he thinks you want to hear and then tell someone else the opposite. I talked to a bunch of people who knew him both as a kid and as an adult.

"He's developed a reputation as a coward. Time was, you could find him right out on the front lines of any demonstration yelling and waving his fist. Now, as soon as push comes to shove, he's out of sight. He can disappear quicker than cigarette smoke, but just like cigarette smoke, he leaves an unpleasant smell behind."

Nick's voice exuded disgust. He never could abide cowardice in any of its many forms.

"Jeez Nick, why don't you just come right out and tell me what you're thinking," I chided.

He ignored me and continued, "One of his cute little tricks goes like this: Suppose you got a little business in the area. Dewayne will stop by to sell you advertising space in the Sentinel. The rates he quotes are just a tad higher than the published ones."

I reached for a fresh pencil and continued transcribing his oral report.

"Now, your first impulse is to throw him out on his can, right? That's when he mentions that an unfriendly story in the Sentinel could just possibly put you out of business."

My right hand flew over the yellow legal pad I used for taking notes. Nick kept on talking.

"Blackmail, huh?" I said.

"On the other hand, he tells you, businesses who advertise in the Sentinel are treated quite well by both the reporting and editorial staff," Nick said.

Jeanetta's choice of boyfriends left me less than impressed with her judgment of character.

"Near as I can tell, the so-and-so is picking up an extra couple of grand a month from his little enterprise."

I continued making notes while Nick continued talking, "Now, here's what I can't figure. What does he do with the money? He drives a crappy little ten year old Nissan with the wheels about falling off. He dresses like he crawled out of a Goodwill donation box. He has few friends and doesn't go clubbing."

I nodded agreement again, remembering the little rust bucket parked alongside Issac's ride.

"It looks like the s.o.b. has only one hobby: Jeanetta. And hell, nobody's ever even seen the two of them holding hands, let alone canoodling."

I couldn't let it pass, "Canoodling?"

"Yeah, canoodling. I'm trying to clean up my language a bit. My present lady doesn't like gutter talk. Want me to be more graphic?"

"No, Nick, that's OK. Keep checking, and see if you can find what he does with his money."

My next stop was Will's office. He was working at his computer terminal and welcomed the interruption. I brought him up to date with my efforts. "I had a nice little sit down with Danny the Dude. He is amenable to giving up his old friend, Mr. Mosticello, to the minions of the law."

Will grunted, "Honor among thieves and all that." He pushed himself away from the keyboard and turned, facing me across his desk.

"He just wants guarantees that there won't be any legal repercussions from his man's actions."

"You did tell him that we could offer no such guarantees," Will commented.

"Of course."

He opened a manila folder on his desk, but didn't refer to it, speaking from memory, "On a different but just maybe related note: we searched high and low around here and interviewed anyone we could find. Whoever took that potshot at you left no trace."

"Any idea where the shot originated?" I asked.

"The trajectory indicated that it came from an alleyway between the old shoe store and the abandoned bakery across the street. Beyond that, we have nothing."

He slid the folder in my direction so that I could see the drawings of the trajectory line.

"Why would anyone want to shoot at me with a pellet gun when something like a 30-06 would be sure to do a better job?"

"Maybe they wanted to avoid being located by the sound of the gunshot," Will offered.

"If so, it worked," I contributed.

I went back to my office to catch up on the paperwork associated with the investigation.

The light on my intercom blinked. "Nick, Detective Todd is on line three," Pamula informed me.

Now that was a surprise. What could the taciturn half of the dynamic duo of investigation have to say to me? Curious, I answered, "O'Connor here."

"O'Connor, I have it on good authority that a very highly placed member of the city administration would consider himself to be in your debt if you would drop the junkyard investigation."

I was flabbergasted. Not only at the offer, but at the stupidity of it. "Go on," I said, while making sure that the digital recording feature of the phone was on and working.

The voice on the other end simply said, "There are many city contracted job sites that need uniformed guards. Maybe a lot of those jobs could come your way."

He then said, "Whatever you decide to do, keep in mind that all debts are repaid." The line went dead.

A quick check of the caller ID showed that aggravating display, "Number unavailable."

There was a light tap on my door. It was Pamula. She entered and closed the door behind her. She said, "Detectives Shallenberger and Todd are in the lounge. They arrived during your last phone conversation and have been waiting to see you."

Curiouser and curiouser. "Show them in."

I played the tape for the detectives. It was amusing to see how the exact same emotion was producing different results in the two men.

Shallenberger reddened to the point that I thought his head was going to go the way of a champagne cork. Todd, on the other hand, paled almost to the point of invisibility.

"This is going too far," said Shallenberger. Todd, ever the recalcitrant, clamped his lips and nodded agreement.

As a means of pouring gasoline on the fire of their emotions I mentioned the obvious fact that someone seemed to want to make their lives less than trouble free. Further, how fortuitous it was that they were in the lobby area as I was taking the call or I might have misgivings about their intentions vis-à-vis the investigation.

They departed our offices looking like they were on a mission. They didn't even mention the reason for their visit.

Now that the waters were getting murkier and murkier, I did the only sensible thing I could think of: I had dinner with Beth.

While the pair of us were enjoying a splendid Italian dinner at an out-of-the way restaurant twenty miles east of the city, Beth's cell phone rang.

She apologized for forgetting to turn it off and, after answering it, handed it to me, saying, "It's for you."

"O'Connor here."

It was Nick. He had tracked down what Dewayne was doing with his money.

"He's the laughing stock of Wilkinsburg. It turns out that he is donating all the money he can get his hands on to a group called the Keepers of the Koran."

Eventually I returned home to find another message on my answering machine. "I won't miss next time."

# CHAPTER 16 - CHESS ANYONE?

Tuesday morning. The only good thing about Tuesday is that it isn't Monday.

Checked my machine when I got to the office and there were two more messages from Jacquie, giving me both her home and cell numbers,

Brewed myself some coffee and tried to catch-up on my mail, newspapers, and magazines that had been piling up. It wasn't that successful an endeavor as I skimmed everything and rapidly transferred the pile of paper on my desk to a crushed wad of paper in the wastebasket. At least it killed an hour.

Eleven AM. OK, it's late enough to call Miss Howard.

"Hello, Jacquie? It's PT O'Connor returning your call. What's up?"

Concern was evident in her melodious voice.

"Mr. O'Connor, I'm so glad you called back. It's my sister Jeanetta. I'm worried about her. Is there some place we can meet and talk?"

I left it up to her and she suggested lunch at an well known restaurant in Squirrel Hill.

I met her at a place not far from the intersection of Forbes and Murray Avenues that the locals call the Squirrel Cage. It is a friendly neighborhood bar and grill that is a favorite of the white and blue collar lunch crowd in the area.

I ordered a hearty Reuben with a side of chips and kosher dill pickles while she opted for a tossed salad.

I bit into my sandwich appreciatively, remembering that I was overdue for lunch. Wiping a horseradish and mustard caused tear from the corner of my eye, I asked her something that had been on my mind. "Jacquie, why do you want to talk with me instead of Will, your mom, or even Uncle Clarence?"

She explained that Jeanetta was the baby of the family and she felt protective toward her and didn't want to tell Will anything that would reflect poorly on her.

"So you want to filter the bad news though me," I said and she nodded while toying with her salad.

Two PM. I was back at the office discussing my luncheon date with Will.

"Jeanetta is scared to death that her sister is being taking advantage of. She said that she has found out that Jacquie has been funneling money to Dewayne. Not just the odd twenty or fifty: we're talking thousands of dollars.

"She's been cashing in savings bonds, cleaning-out her cash accounts and god knows what else."

"Hmmm, looks like someone had better have a talk with our young gentleman."

"Hmmm, looks like I'm elected."

"Hmmm, right."

I wasn't sure what, exactly, I was going to say, but the gist of it had formed in my mind even before consulting Will.

It was still relatively early, so I called Dewayne on the phone and asked him if I could have a word with him over dinner. He agreed and suggested a Chinese Restaurant on Penn Avenue in Wilkinsburg.

Wilkinsburg is an enigma. It is a dry community that has neither bars, taverns, nor other establishments that dispense alcoholic beverages. It also once boasted the nickname of, "Town of Churches."

While alcoholic beverages are still unavailable legally, it is now a hotbed of urban crime and decay. The streets are a battleground between warring factions and not just after dark. Shootings are commonplace and tall reddish-blonde white guys are an endangered species there.

I made a few other phone calls and got to the restaurant a little after six. It was a storefront place with dark painted booths along the left wall and tables scattered throughout the rest of the dining room. The kitchen was in the back. Dewayne was in the rearmost booth and waved me over. There were maybe six or eight other diners in the place.

I sat down facing Dewayne with my back to the door. I'm always uncomfortable when my back is to the door.

He exhibited a grimace that I took for a smile, extended his limp hand and said, "What's on your mind, Mr. O'Connor?"

Before I could reply, a chubby little oriental woman was at our table providing us with green tea and taking our dinner orders.

"Well, Dewayne, you know what I do for a living, right? I've been doing some checking and have found out a few things that could use a little clearing-up."

He took a sip of tea and eyed me over the cup before putting it down.

"Such as?"

Oh no, it irks me when someone decides to play it cute.

"Such as the money you have been weaseling out of Jeanetta. For starters. Any explanation would be greatly appreciated."

He smirked as he replied, "Jeanetta is a big girl now and, to the best of my knowledge, she is allowed to do what she wishes with her own money. If she feels sufficiently dedicated to the Cause, so be it."

My turn to sip some green tea. When I returned the cup to its saucer, I took care to enunciate each and every word carefully, so that there would be no mistaking my meaning.

"That's not an explanation. I am not going to play word games with you. Jeanetta is the granddaughter of a person whom I greatly admire. If anything untoward should happen to her, physically, mentally or emotionally, I will hold you personally responsible. Understand?"

That pasted on smile of his never wavered as he said, "Perfectly, Mr. PT. Now let me tell you something. The white race that you are part of, under the guise of a so-called religion called Christianity, has been practicing genocide on both people of color and people of other beliefs for over one thousand years."

I countered, "And what is it that you have been practicing on people of color with your little advertisement scam at the Sentinel?"

The smile was no longer evident and his voice became louder as it increased in stridency. He continued without skipping a beat, as though he were reading from a script.

"Your church-sanctioned crusades resulted in the near elimination of everything Mohammedan in the world. It has taken that thousand years to recover and now we are ready."

"Ready for what, Dewayne?" I figured to let him finish parroting whatever demagogue was influencing him at the present. Then, just maybe, we could talk.

"We are ready to take revenge for centuries of oppression. My Arab brethren have been crushed under the yoke of oil sheiks while my East Indian brethren have slaved under the direction of the Spice Cartel. My South African brothers die to put pretty stones on the fingers of rich white women. My own family was torn from its African roots and forced to toil as slaves on your cotton and tobacco plantations."

His diatribe was starting to draw the attention of other patrons as he went on.

"Now, I have dedicated my life and my soul to the forthcoming jihad which will, once and for all, eliminate all who have oppressed and opposed us from this earth.

"And, you. You have the unmitigated gall to question the motives of a disciple who has converted to our cause."

He was really into it now.

"You say that you will hold me responsible. Nay- nay- I say that it I who hold you responsible. Responsible for the uncounted murders of true believers. For which there can be only one penalty: Death!"

He punctuated that last word by slamming a fist down on the table, rattling tea cups and silverware and capturing my full attention.

Belatedly, I sensed movement to my right and a large black man slid into the booth beside me, pushing me across the bench to my left. I could feel an object pressing against my ribs as the gentleman muttered, "Shut up. Be quiet and come with us."

An associate of his slid onto the bench directly across from me alongside Dewayne. He wasn't gifted with a particularly large frame and his complexion was rather sallow for a man of color. The pistol that he surreptitiously displayed made up for any of his shortcomings as he greeted me with a mirthless smile in dire need of dental attention.

Thank God that I believed in the motto of the United States Coast Guard, "Semper Paratus."

Wearing a long raincoat off the shoulders, a tall muscular fellow walked by our booth headed to the kitchen area. He stopped at our booth and rested a bluish-black cylindrical object with a 12 gauge bore against the neck of the man sitting next to me, and said, "Stalemate."

"'Bout time, Nick."

"You're welcome, PT."

Another of our operatives, LeBlanc by name, came over to the table, letting his jacket slide slightly to the side so that Dewayne and his friend could see the Uzi dangling from the lanyard over his shoulder. It was pointing at them.

"PT, would you please be kind enough to relieve that man of his hardware?" I think it was Nick that made the request.

I simply put out my hand and a surprisingly compact semi-automatic pistol found its way into it. The fellow across the table from me handed his, butt-first, to Carlos. It was similar, but not identical, to the one in my hand.

In response to a request of Nick's, the gentleman next to me slid out of the booth, allowing me to slide out also. He then returned to his place across from Dewayne.

I placed what I considered a sufficient amount of money on the table and said, "Dinner is on me."

Then, making sure that I had his undivided attention, I leaned over and carefully informed, "Remember what I said, Dewayne: Physically, mentally or emotionally. Good day."

On our way out I noticed a group of muscular young men lounging around the entrance to the restaurant. Something about them struck a familiar chord.

*

I definitely didn't want to have the guns in my possession any longer than absolutely necessary, they were that hot. As soon as I returned to the office I made a phone call and persuaded Exie to stop by and pick up the confiscated guns. I explained the circumstances that brought them into my hands, omitting any reference to Dewayne.

"PT, do you know what you have here?"

"Yeah, a couple of guns that are no longer on the street."

Knowing that the outside of the pistols had already been wiped clean, he turned one over in his hands examining it.

He then said, "What you have here is a pair of pistols. The first one is a Russian Tokarev 7.62 by 25 semiautomatic. Coincidentally, a truckload of these was hijacked in the northern New Jersey area and is suspected of having found its way into the hands of militant folk of the Middle East variety."

My turn to be surprised. I thought the Keepers of the Koran were strictly a local organization.

As I inspected the deadly piece of steel the thought crossed my mind that this little junkyard caper was getting out of hand.

Exie hefted the other one in his hand, then set it down on the desk and said, "Unless I am mistaken, this other little piece doesn't even exist."

It both felt and looked as though it had substance to me so I asked him to explain.

He replied, "Well this little .380 automatic is the same make and caliber as one that was supposed to have been sent to the bowels of a steel blast furnace by Detectives Shallenberger and Todd. Now it seems as though this nonexistent gun has killed at least one man and threatened another, namely you."

I was tempted to explain to Exie that guns neither kill nor threaten people, people do. I decided to spare him this late night parroting of NRA philosophy, whether I believed in it or not.

We then did a little paperwork concerning exactly how those guns came into my possession and Exie departed with the guns.

Before leaving, he cautioned me, "Keep this under your hat for the time being, at least until a buddy of mine at the crime lab can verify my suspicions."

I assured him that, as far as I was concerned, mum's the word.

There was one bright spot in my day. When I arrived home, there was no nasty little message on my machine to greet me.

# CHAPTER 17 - HUMP DAY

I was too wired up to get much in the way of sleep. Even a five-mile run along the riverbank didn't help unwind the tension. All a hot shower did was to wash off the stink. As a result I got to the office a bit earlier than is my custom. I'd better watch out. Getting in early was starting to be my custom.

Pamula indicated with a raised eyebrow and a nod of her head that Will wanted to see me. As soon as I had a steaming mug of coffee in my hand, I went in to his office.

"What's up, Will?"

"PT, you think rattling everybody's cage is such a wise idea? You know, you can get killed. Then where'll I find someone to replace you? You're one of a kind, you know."

I took a sip of my morning coffee and confessed, "I'll tell you, Will, I didn't know that Jeanetta's boyfriend was into such heavy stuff. I thought that, at the most, I was going to need to get out of a sticky situation."

It wasn't easy, but I managed to slip in another sip of coffee before continuing, "At the worst, I figured some trouble with street punks. That's why I had the backup on the scene. And, boy was I glad they were there."

I set the mug down on a conveniently placed coaster on the side table and went on, "But now I've got some other worries. For instance: does Jeanetta know what her boyfriend is into? These people aren't above kidnapping and murder to support their cause. Hell, these are the same kind of people that are running around doing suicide bombings."

Once that first surge of half-caffeinated hot liquid made its way into my system, I was ready for a pastry.

"How does all this tie in to a simple little junkyard take-over?" I questioned, powdered sugar snowing on my shirt.

Will shoved a box of tissues in my direction as an incentive to clean up, "OK, slow down, PT. I've done some checking myself. This so-called jihad that Dewayne was speaking of exists primarily in his head and the heads of the unfortunate few that he follows. I think that the poor fellow has been brain washed to believe all that crap he espouses."

I wiped away the traces of sugar, got another sip of coffee and opined, "Brain washed or not, the guns those guys were packing weren't imaginary."

"Yeah, well I understand that the hardware you, Nick and LeBlanc were carrying wasn't a figment of someone's imagination, either. Besides, if those guys really believed in martyrdom for martyrdom's sake, you wouldn't be here now."

"Yeah, and those guys would have learned an alternate definition for the word, 'holy,'" I retorted.

Will really caught my attention when he said, "Let's consider the possibility that Dewayne is a victim of a well-played con."

A couple rays of light were starting to penetrate my consciousness.

"OK, then how do Danny, Wallace and Vivien figure into this?"

"They don't."

More rays.

"And Issac?"

"He doesn't."

"And Unk?"

"He's the pivot point of this whole damn thing. Remember, ninety-nine times out of a hundred, the action will take place around the source of money. For different reasons to different people, Uncle Clarence represents wealth. Above all else, we've got to protect him."

As I returned to my office, I felt my excitement building. I could sense the conspiracy starting to crumble. I knew that we had nearly all the pieces of the puzzle and only had to assemble them in a coherent form. One thing that stood out was the murder of McClymonds. It didn't fit in with anything else.

I sat at my desk trying to order my thoughts about the case. I pulled a chain of differently colored karabiners from my bottom left drawer and separated them into individual links. I assigned a different part of the case to each link. I thought that by rearranging the links and linking different facts together, it might help me to see the case from a different perspective.

The buzz of my intercom jolted me back to reality.

"PT, Line three. City's finest."

Karabiners into clues into links into who knew what…thanking God for the interruption I picked up the receiver and spoke into it.

"Hello, PT O'Connor here. What can I do for you?"

"O'Connor- Shallenberger here. Where in the hell did you get those pistols?"

How in the name of all that's good and holy did Shallenberger get his hands on the pieces I'd handed over to Exie? I replied, "I don't know what you're talking about."

"That's not good enough, O'Connor. Ballistics testing shows that one of these pistols was used in at least one homicide in this jurisdiction."

Damn it. I'd love to know what Exie was up to with this. It looked like I wasn't going to have the chance to find out. Shallenberger continued, "You got some 'splaining to do, friend. I'll be right over to hear what you have to say. Consider this to be an advance warning."

"Thanks, friend," I replied to a severed connection. He must've been already on his way.

I checked with Will as to whether or not to get a lawyer here before Shallenberger arrived. We decided to wait and see.

True to his word, Shallenberger was leaning on the front door buzzer in less than a half-hour. His partner wasn't with him. That alone seemed unusual.

As soon as Pamula buzzed him in, he rushed straight back to my office as though the devil was on his tail. He helped himself to a mug of coffee, threw his straw hat on a chair, and sitting on a corner of my desk said, "O'Connor, I ducked out on Manny. I figure that this conversation doesn't need witnesses. This way it'll be off the record."

I nodded to indicate my agreement with staying off the record.

He sipped at the coffee with gusto. Then, with concern in his voice, said, "Listen up. The item we were discussing – that you know nothing about – puts you in a bad light. Either you or the last guy before you to hold that gun killed McClymonds."

I gave a passing thought to mentioning that he and Todd had signed on the dotted line for the item in question, but thought I'd hold that back, for now. Knowing that it wasn't me who drilled McClymonds, I said so.

Shallenberger just shook his head like a dog trying to rid himself of excess water and went on, "That isn't all. One of the damn things matches bullets dug out of a wall at a bank robbery, and its serial numbers shows it was part of a truck shipment hijacked in New Jersey. This will be getting Federal attention, since the hijacking falls under ATF jurisdiction."

He carefully placed the coffee mug on a napkin so that it wouldn't mar my desk.

"When one of the early suspects in a murder case turns up with the murder weapon, it doesn't contribute to his innocence," He said.

I cocked my head to one side and asked, "Why are you telling me all this? Especially if I am a suspect?"

Shallenberger alighted from my desk, walked to the door as though to insure that we wouldn't be overheard and returned to my desk. Both hands resting on the front of the desk, he leaned over, and in a conspiratorial tone said, "Listen, kid, when I first started on this case I figured you for a wise guy. Now I see that you are a stand-up sort. I can't tell you why, but I don't think that you have anything to do with McClymond's murder. Furthermore, there are certain people who are fitting you for a frame for that murder. I won't stand for that on my watch."

I appreciated his candor and told him so. But I still had no idea why he was confiding in me. Because of this, or maybe in spite of this, I still saw no reason to trust him and told him so.

He answered by taking a cell phone from his pocket, dialing it, and waiting for an answer. When he got one, he mumbled a sentence or two into the receiver and handed it to me.

I said, "Yeah?"

The voice on the other end, well known to me said, "The man with you is OK. Trust him like you would me."

In light of Exie's endorsement, I leveled with Shallenberger and told him most of what had happened the previous evening.

He was all fired up to go out and start making arrests, but I was able to dissuade him.

"After all," I explained, "wouldn't it be neater to clean this up in a controlled environment?"

We let it stand at that, agreeing to wait until we were able to wrap up the whole kit and kaboodle in one neat package.

Then it was over to Will's office to bring him up to speed.

Later, while I was ruminating about the case, something dawned on me: I had spoken with all the principals in the case with the exception of the one guy who was there at the very start: Armand Mosticello. For some reason his presence hadn't so much as made a ripple on the pond of this whole thing.

I thought I'd better have a talk with the bag man I called Danny Saint Martin.

Jeez, and it was barely noon.

# CHAPTER 18 - RINKY REVISITED

I called Mr. Saint Martin using one of my disposable cell phones and we discussed items of mutual interest, especially that area dealing with persons of murderous intent. We felt that it would be advantageous for each of us to do our utmost to prevent future bloodshed, particularly our own.

I explained how it would be of paramount importance to get the facts as observed by Mr. Mosticello into the mix. Danny agreed and mentioned the name of an out-of-the way tavern a few miles north east of the city. He said that Armand Mosticello just might be there at about three that very afternoon.

The place was one of those falling-down Insulbrick-sided two-story affairs so common in the semi-rural rust belt areas of Western Pennsylvania. Located on a potholed two lane side road in the hilly countryside, it announced its presence with a faded, rusted sign on a pole near the road that simply said, "Bar." Lined up at the front of the building like horses to a trough were a half-dozen four- wheel-drive pickup trucks in various states of disrepair. A lone Buick sedan was nestled up to one side of the ramshackle roadhouse.

The thought crossed my mind that my belt buckle would be haute couture in these environs.

A plume of dust announced my arrival when I parked alongside the Buick. I left the two sedans to keep each other company while I was inside.

The darkened interior, redolent of stale beer and cigarette smoke, had little islands of light that indicated the location of tables scattered around that part of the interior not occupied by the fifteen foot square bar.

Off to the left of the entrance I could see the requisite pair of pinball machines, flanked by the jukebox on one side and the men's room on the other.

The owners of five of the trucks clustered at one corner of the bar. The owner of the sixth was on the other side of the bar. They were concentrating on satisfying their liquid needs. My quarry, dimly illuminated at the edge of one of the islands of light, sat nervously alone. I got a bottled beer and sat opposite him at the chrome and Formica table farthest from the entrance.

Little beads of sweat danced between his hairline and eyebrows in defiance of the refrigeration-like air conditioning.

"Are you O'Connor?"

"I am if you're Mosticello," I replied.

He drew circles in the puddle caused by his whiskey and ginger ale.

"What do you want?" Fear flickered in his eyes.

I countered his question with one of my own. "Where have you been lately?"

His eyes were constantly darting around the bar as though he were trying to keep track of everyone and everything in the place simultaneously. He answered my query with two words, "Hiding out."

Boy, was I glad I wasn't being paid by the word. I tried again to kick the conversation into gear.

"Hiding out from whom? The police?"

He took a sip of his drink, wiped his mouth with the back of his hand, checked the bunch at the bar and said, "I don't know who in the hell I'm hiding from. Somebody killed Josh and I think I'm next. And, I don't know why or who."

I could almost hear his nerves thrumming with tension. Sweat beaded on his upper lip and he had that clammy look exhibited by victims of violent crimes.

Sometimes it's unpleasant to watch a man fold up and cave in. This wasn't one of those times. I had no compassion for Mosticello. He had a malady common to those who prey on the weak. It goes by the name of cowardice.

"Listen up. I need to know everything that happened that night when McClymonds got whacked. You know that you have clearance from Saint Martin to level with me, so you might as well spill it all." I didn't know that this last was true. I just threw it in on the off chance.

It worked. He must've been waiting all this time for a father confessor, because he opened the floodgates.

A good bit of what he said wasn't news because Beth and Pamula had doped it out.

"Ya see, me and Josh was told to lean on the old black guy for Danny to be able to buy his place on the cheap. Ya know what I mean?"

That wasn't much in the way of news to me and I told him so.

Rinky (I'm sorry, but I couldn't think of him by any other name) continued. He said that, on the night that they were going to, in his words, "Knock some sense into the yard worker," I showed-up and screwed up their plans.

As they were leaving the wreck, Dinky, that is Josh, remarked that he thought he recognized the concerned citizen from somewhere. When he realized that the, "concerned citizen," was none other than yours truly, they made an immediate U-turn and returned to the scene. By that time, the cluster of flashing lights on the road prevented them from doing bodily harm to me.

As he told me this, he winced as though he expected me to retaliate on the spot. I gave him my most winsome smile and told him that there was no harm done. Somewhere in the dim recesses of my consciousness was an urge to reunite him with the lost billy, but I managed to stifle it.

We had our drinks refreshed (my treat) and he went on.

The next day, Rinky had me made from the time I started making the door-to-door survey in his little tight-knit neighborhood. Either he or his mom had me in sight nearly nonstop from the time I first set foot on their block. So much for unwitting maternal participation.

Rinky continued, "A phone call to Danny and we had you set up for the rest of the day. We took a ride all over the south hills. What you didn't know was that we were delivering pamphlets and posters about the upcoming Italian Day at Kennywood Amusement Park to all the politicos and law enforcement types we could think of throughout the South Hills." Satisfaction with a job well done caused him to be a bit more ebullient. He was getting into it now.

In the meantime, someone had fed a handful of quarters to the jukebox, and the establishment filled with the sounds of a steel guitar and a musically challenged voice. It was difficult to determine which was whining louder, the guitar or the singer. In either case I had to lean closer to Rinky to hear what he was saying.

"Yeah, we really had you going there. We were supposed to keep you occupied until Danny got some business out of the way."

"Well then, how in the hell did I wind up with lumps, if all you were supposed to do was to keep me busy?" I asked, a bit more forcible than I'd intended.

He flinched and pushed back in his chair for distance before saying, "It wasn't us that roughed you up. It was someone else. First thing we knew something was up was when you and some big black car tangled near the bridge.

"We turned around to see what had happened. When we got back there, you were lying on the ground outside your car. Josh got out to see what was happening and next thing I knew, the front of his head got blown away by a shot from behind.

"I don't remember nothing else from that night except that I got the hell out of there as fast as I could. I swear on my mother's grave that I'm telling the truth."

I didn't mention that his mother wasn't in one yet as I said, "I know that, you know that. But, the way it's set to go down, the police won't know that.

"Now, I can clear you, but I haven't really got any incentive for doing so. After all, you guys were trying to kill me, too."

"No, Mr. O'Connor, I swear that I had nothing to do with…"

I interrupted with, "Enough swearing for one day. I not only know where the murder weapon is, but I can put it in either your hand or someone else's hand at the time of the murder."

Damn. If he was telling the truth, and I had no reason to doubt him, I was back to square one. If he and Dinky weren't trying to kill me that night, someone else was involved. Great.

"If you want it to be someone else's hand, I need better information from you. I want to know why Danny wants a junkyard and I want to know what his connection is with Universal Steel."

He said he didn't know for sure, but thought that he might need one for disposing of chop shop cars.

A chop shop is a place where stolen vehicles are dismantled for their parts. The individual parts from a five year old Chevy are more valuable than a whole brand-new one.

When a car is completely dismantled, the chop shop is left with frame and uni-body parts that have to be discarded in such a way that the serial numbers don't come back to bite the thief. A junkyard with a car crusher would be invaluable to a stolen car ring.

That may have been all that Rinky could figure, but I thought that a larger pot of gold was at the end of Danny's rainbow.

We discussed a few more things, and a half-hour later found me back on Route 28 heading south with a head full of undigested information and a promise from Armand that he would take care to keep his mother out of trouble.

I, in turn promised him that he was off the hook for the murder. I was as truthful with him as he was with me.

It was still early enough for me to get into some trouble.

Back at the office, I organized the information that Armand had volunteered. His convoluted tale of woe actually included two or three things that I was unaware of.

That damn chirp or beep or whatever coming from the phone interrupted my train of thought. Everyone else was gone for the day and I was tempted to just let it ring until it switched over to Will's condo. That is, until I saw the caller ID, "Southside Scrap Works."

I picked up the receiver and said, "W.E.B. Enterprises."

"PT, is that you?" It was Uncle Clarence.

"Sure is. What can I do for you, Unk?"

"Jeanetta's been kidnapped. Someone's holding her for ransom. If I don't come up with a half million dollars in forty-eight hours, she'll be killed."

I put everything else on the back burner and started setting things in motion. The first call was to Will.

# CHAPTER 19 - LITTLE GIRL LOST

Friday morning promised another hot and sticky day for the city. After convening a war council at the office and sending out operatives in all possible directions, all we could do was wait for developments. Nothing of import had happened since I received Unk's call Thursday evening.

We all had that coiled spring feeling. That one that comes when every bit of your being is ready for whatever happens whenever it happens. As a result of being at that high state of readiness for a protracted period of time, we felt its effects. Everyone had jangled nerves, even without the stimulus of caffeine. Our eyes were gritty from poring over pages of reports, hoping for a break. Our hands twitched from grabbing at air every time the phone rang, desperately wanting news. Hoping for good news and needing any news, just to break the tension.

Sometimes, even though it's nerve wracking, no news is good news. The radio frequency scanners indicated that neither the media nor the police had picked up on the kidnapping. That was good news in a negative sort of way.

Will, being Will didn't waste time with could've, would've, or should've. Remonstration wasn't needed, action was. Markers were pulled in from all over.

Before the man assigned to keep watch over her had even made his complete report, operatives were fanning out trying to locate Dewayne Collins. He should know where Jeanetta had gotten to. Unfortunately, it seemed as though he had disappeared off the face of the earth. Operatives reported in one after the other with negative results on his office, apartment, and hangouts. Nobody had gotten a whiff of him since sometime around noon Thursday.

"It looks like Jeanetta has deliberately dumped the protective tail we had put on her," I observed unnecessarily.

Our man reported that he had followed her all over the Squirrel Hill shopping district for a couple of hours. He said she visited every shoe store and boutique in a four- block area. His only break came when she stopped at a Peking style oriental restaurant on Murray Avenue for a late lunch. Our man was able to grab a sandwich and an iced tea at a deli across the street.

When she finished her lunch, she walked the few blocks uphill to Forbes Avenue and entered a dry cleaner's. After a few minutes, he went in to check and she was nowhere in sight. The counter clerk said that she had told her that her ex-boyfriend was bothering her and asked if there was a back way out.

She left the dry cleaner's through the rear door where the delivery vans pick up and drop off clothing. She had only a five, or six minute head start, but it was enough. She was gone.

That was at 4 PM, about the same time I was winding down my conversation with Rinky.

At 4:45 PM, the phone at the junkyard rang. Clarence Reynolds answered it. The conversation was short and one sided. Mr. Reynolds told Will and me that it went like this:

"We have your granddaughter. She is alive for the time being. You can have her back for a half-million dollars. You have forty-eight hours. We will be in touch with instructions. Allah Aakbar!"

The caller then broke the connection.

One thing was obvious to us all. Whether or not she was cooperating, she was in danger. Kidnappers seldom leave a victim behind to identify them.

We went over everything again.

Rubbing the sleep from her eyes, Beth commented, not for the first time, "Her lying sack of canine excrement of a boyfriend is in it up to his turkey wattle neck."

Pamula, drumming on the desktop with her fingernails replied, "His kind are survivors. He's got to be in hiding somewhere. And, I think I just might know where. Come on Beth, let's go."

She scooped up her purse, stuffed a little S&W Escort .22 automatic somewhere in her bodice region, grabbed a travel mug of coffee, and headed for the door.

Beth caught her at the door, similarly equipped with a purse and a hot mug of coffee. Her artillery was likewise demurely concealed somewhere on her athletic frame.

They paused at the door in response to Will's bellow, "Hey!

Where're you two going?"

Pamula called back through the closing door, "Somewhere where you lugs would stick out like clowns at a funeral. We'll be back in an hour."

We just looked at one another and shrugged our shoulders. That the women were up to something there was no doubt. That it involved Dewayne Collins there was equally no doubt. Knowing the proclivity of both Pamula and Beth for solving problems expeditiously and satisfactorily, we turned our attention to other things.

Morning rush hour was over, so the radio and TV stations stopped their news, weather and traffic updates every ten minutes and returned to entertainment programming.

Celeste and Jacqui were sitting on the edges of their chairs facing Uncle Clarence. The three of them were silently moving their lips as though in prayer.

Will had taken care of routing Unk's home and office phones, and Celeste's home phone to our office console. Call forwarding is a wonderful thing. I'm not so sure about call waiting.

The birdlike chirp of the telephone shattered the silence as well as the prayer vigil.

Motioning for silence, Will pointed to Unk as he silently counted backwards from three to zero and then hit the button activating the speaker phone.

Unk answered, "Hello?"

"Instructions for delivery of the money have been left in the mailbox at your place of business." The caller hung up.

Jacqui had moved around to the back of Will's desk and was staring at the telephone console in disbelief. Disbelief of what I wasn't sure. Maybe that such evil people inhabited her previously serene world.

Will, relieved that a course of action had broken the tension, started barking orders.

"Jack, head over to the scrapyard and check the mailbox. PT, call Nick, and get him back here. Call in whoever is checking on Jeanetta's hangouts, we're going to need some manpower."

"Uncle Will? Uncle Will. UNCLE WILL!" All activity stopped and we all looked at Jacqui. People seldom yelled to get Will's attention and Jacqui had never raised her voice in our presence before.

Celeste found her voice first and asked her daughter "What's the matter honey?"

Jacqui pointed at the phone console and said, "Look. Look at the caller ID."

Will, skeptical, walked around his desk saying, "Naw, I don't think so. Nobody could be that stupid."

Everyone gathered around the telephone display. There it was for all to see, "The Royal Motel. 412 555 1234."

Six different people. Multiple opinions on how to act.

Jacqui didn't offer an opinion. She had done her part.

Everyone talked at once hearing only their own voice and opinion:

I contributed to the confusion by saying, "Just because the call originated from the motel doesn't mean that they're at the motel now."

"Yeah, maybe they did it on purpose to throw us off," Jack agreed.

"Maybe the call didn't come from the motel at all: they might have one of those thingies that'll change your caller ID," said one of the operatives that obviously studied electronic countermeasure manuals.

Unk said, "These guys are revolutionaries, after all."

"They might have a whole army around the place."

"We oughta load-up with some really heavy-duty stuff before we leave." This came from the Uzi toting LeBlanc.

"Yeah, God only knows what weapons they might be packing," someone concurred with his astute observation.

"Will, do you think we should notify the authorities," Celeste asked.

At this point, Beth and Pamula walked through the front door with a decidedly unenthusiastic Dewayne Collins in tow. Beth was applying a painful, but non-lethal finger twist on one of the digits of his left hand. She held that hand behind his back in a less than friendly manner.

Jacqui set aside the morning paper she was unsuccessfully trying to read, and took a menacing step in Collins' direction while asking, "What rock did you find this slug under?"

Beth replied, "Hiding out at University Library of course."

She deposited him in a chair under the baleful eye of Uncle Clarence. Pamula said, "What's up, guys?"

While Uncle Clarence was flexing and unknotting muscles preparatory to asking Dewayne about his granddaughter's location and condition, Pamula and Beth were filled-in on developments.

Pamula immediately cooled all talk of artillery, authorities, and the kidnappers' hi-tech prowess.

"These guys are idiots. Dangerous idiots. But idiots just the same. Don't over think it."

Since McKees Rocks was over halfway to the Royal Motel, I made a quick phone call to Jim Shepherd. He agreed to have some of his boys pave the way for us.

In the next few minutes Uncle Clarence garnered some information from Dewayne concerning the so-called kidnapping plot. It was Dewayne's contention that Jeanetta was in no danger.

Wiping tears from his eyes after being slapped a few times across the face by Uncle Clarence, he sniveled, "I wouldn't do any thing that would hurt her."

Uncle Clarence dismissed him with a snort of disgust. "How can you trust anything from a punk that breaks down crying from a couple of bitch slaps?"

Celeste cocked an eyebrow at Unk's untoward use of an epithet. It wasn't like him.

Will waved a fist in Collins's direction and simply said, "Get him out of here."

Dewayne fled into the morning sunlight.

Shortly thereafter, three carloads of W.E.B.'s best agents hit the road heading for the Royal Motel on Route 60. Will was in the lead car with two men and I was in the tail car with Unk and one more agent. In spite of the circumstances, because of the time of day and the proliferation of road reconstruction, traffic crawled. We were forced to take a somewhat leisurely route through the city.

Ten minutes into the trip, my cell phone chirped. It was Will calling from the lead car.

"PT, a change of plans. I'll continue on. You and everybody else return to the office. Pamula just called and told me that Jeanetta's escaped. We will pick her up at the Eat 'n Park Restaurant near the motel. See you back at the office in an hour."

Speculation ran wild at the office until Will returned around noon.

Tears running down his face, Uncle Clarence swept up his granddaughter into his arms. Truth be told, there were tears enough for everyone to have a measure. Celeste and Uncle Clarence were effusive in their gratitude.

Jeanetta and Jacquetta pirouetted around each other with squeals of delight. All in all it was an ecstatic family reunion. Will however, seemed less than one hundred percent enthusiastic at the present turn of events.

Eventually things settled down and the Howard family and Uncle Clarence left for home and rest.

Will thanked everyone for their help and sent the operatives home with instructions to get some well-deserved rest and to stay near their telephones.

Finally, everyone else had left. Will, Pamula, Beth and I gathered around Will's Desk.

I munched on a bit of doughnut left over from the vigil and asked, "What's up boss? You don't look happy."

Will slammed his palm down flat on his desk and said, "If she had a daddy, Jeanetta is one little bitch that ought to be getting her ass whupped right about now."

Pamula acknowledged his aggravation by setting her cup of tea on the edge of his desk, quizzically raising her right eyebrow and waiting for him to go on. Which he did.

"The little so and so was in on it from the beginning. As far as she was concerned, it was all a lark. She thought that she was in training to be an undercover agent for the revolution that will never come.

"She didn't even know she was being held hostage until I told her."

Will was flabbergasted. I guess he didn't have much experience with impressionable youngsters.

He took a quick swig of his iced tea and continued, "She thought she was being sequestered at the motel for training. The motley crew that comprised the Keepers of the Koran gave her a bunch of propaganda pamphlets and guerrilla manuals to study."

Pamula went around behind Will and tried to knead the tension out of him by massaging his neck and shoulder muscles. I gave Beth a beseeching look. She responded by rubbing her own neck and silently mouthing, "In your dreams, buddy."

Will related, "Jeanetta said that around eight in the morning one of the young women disciples of the Keepers went out to get coffee and rolls while the other was taking a shower. By then Jeanetta was bored with the whole program so she left. Just like that. She picked up her purse, walked out the door, and phoned home from the Eat 'n Park for a ride."

Will couldn't contain his disbelief. It was in his expression, his body language, and his voice. Though he wouldn't admit it, there was quite a bit of relief in his countenance too.

"She said that after reading all the anti-US propaganda in the booklets and skimming the guerrilla manuals they provided her, it all just seemed stupid. So she left."

Beth counseled Will, "Don't be too hard on her. She's just a kid."

He said, "Uh-huh," and reached for the phone.

I guessed that the pow-wow was over, at least for the time being.

# CHAPTER 20 - CONFABULATION

A shave, a hot shower, a change of clothes. More than enough to recover from an all-nighter. Yeah – right. Somehow that change of clothes I keep at the office never seems as fresh or comfortable as those at home.

The phone on my desk insisted.

"Yeah."

"Come on, buddy. That's no way for someone to answer a phone." It was Jim Shepherd.

He continued, "Say, pal, remember a few hours ago you asked me to check out the Royal Motel in case you needed some back-up?"

I admitted as much to him while cradling the phone on my shoulder so that I could pour my umpteenth cup of joe for the day.

"Well, me and a couple of my boys paid a visit to the place. We saw a girl matching the description you gave us making a clean walk away from room 103."

I mixed a little nondairy creamer into the brownish-black mess in the cup. "OK, Jim. And?"

A retired cop is still a cop. The excitement of the chase was in his voice. "We watched the room for a while. After a half hour or so, these two douche bags entered the room. So we knocked and announced, "Housekeeping." When they opened the door we rushed them and scooped them up."

It was either the acidic mixture in my cup or what I felt Jim was about to say next. I grimaced and said, "And?"

Jim gleefully replied, "What do you want me to do with them?"

"Uh, hold on a minute, chum. I'll check with Will and get right back to you."

I pushed the hold button, gently set the phone down and banged my forehead on the desk a couple of times to clear my mind. That served two purposes: If I was sleeping it would wake me and if I was awake it would remind me that all this wasn't normal.

Then I walked over to Will's office, poked my head in the doorway and said, "Will?"

He looked up from the papers he was examining and grunted acknowledgment.

"Uh, Boss. Jim Shepherd has captured the Keepers of the Koran and wants to know what to do with them. He's on my line."

Will raised both eyebrows almost to his hairline in an expression of surprise, smiled, waved me to a chair and picked up the phone. He accessed my line and said, "Hello, Jim. Great job, we are all in your debt. Say, if it isn't too much trouble, do you think you can convince our zealous so-called Muslim friends to accompany you to my office?"

He cut the connection and returned his attention to me, saying, "Jim said no problem, he'll be here in an hour or so with Jeanetta's would-be kidnappers."

He then gave me a list of things to do and people to call preparatory to their arrival.

The first of those I'd called arrived less than a half hour later. They were shortly followed by the most reluctant of those I'd contacted. After I assured him that he had not only my, but also Will's guarantee that he would come to no bodily harm while at our office, Dandy Danny Saint Martin dismissed his over muscled chauffeur, telling him that he would call him when he was needed.

I thanked him and escorted him through the lobby to Will's office. He took in the carpeting, paintings and furniture with obvious appreciation.

Just before entering Will's office, he turned to me and said, "This had better be good, O'Connor."

I promised him that he would be entertained and showed him to a comfortable seat in the right rear of the room. A small table was conveniently placed to the left of his chair.

His interest was immediately piqued when he observed Mr. and Mrs. Locke sitting on the opposite side of the room. I equipped him with an extra dry vodka martini sans salad which he raised in a mock toast in the general direction of the Lockes.

Vivian Locke was inordinately preoccupied with her husband, taking pains to ignore Saint Martin's presence.

Jim showed up with my two friends from the Chinese restaurant and two girls that I assumed were their accomplices. A couple of his young boxers also came along to help. One of his protégés was a large and muscular black man whom I recognized.

"Good morning, Issac," I said, "Fancy meeting you here."

"Jim and I go back a long ways," he replied, "When you called him, he called me."

When all was said and done, the leaders of the Jihad, Abdullah and Hakim, were seated in the chairs of honor directly under the baleful gaze of Will Barrett who sat on the other side of his massive desk.

Will toyed with a pencil, turning it over and over between his fingers. He cocked an eye at Jim and said, "Jim, do we have any idea who these clowns are?"

Jim sipped from a large tumbler of fruit juice and ice, indicated the larger of my old friends from the Chinese restaurant, and replied, "This fellow here who calls himself Hakim is really one Lorenzo Walters. He's a small-time hustler from the East End." Walters, a blocky man the color and texture of fresh chocolate syrup made a movement of protest.

He remained in his seat with the able assistance of Issac's hands pushing down on his shoulders.

Jim sat on the corner of Will's desk facing the semi-circle of punks and indicated with a nod of his head the fidgety, skinny guy sitting next to Walters.

"Next, we have Abdulla. His mama calls him William Jones. Everyone else calls him Willie Lump-Lump."

Jim chuckled and said, "It's a toss-up how he got his nickname. It depends on who you talk to. Some say it came from all the lumps he got from the rest of the kids in the neighborhood. Others say it's because his coloration and acne makes his face look like lumpy chicken gravy."

Willie just smiled self-consciously and shrugged his shoulders as though he was apologizing for his existence. He was that kind of guy.

A dark strand of spaghetti with an attitude and a hip-hugging micro-skirt was perched next to Walters. She called herself Morahuni, while her driver's license called her Connie Fredrickson. Her short, corpulent counterpart was wearing a bandanna-type head covering and introduced herself as Rashiksa. Once again, her driver's license disagreed indicating that her name was Mary Jones.

Will rested his chin on his tented fingers and fixed his most rueful expression on the assemblage of miscreants. Sorrowfully swiveling his head from one side to the other, he said, "What are we going to do with you?"

Walters made a movement of his head and lips as if to reply, but Will waved him off and continued, "At least one of you is guilty of murder. The rest are kidnappers, terrorists, thieves and conspirators, just for starters."

Before anyone could move, the strand of spaghetti jumped up and round-housed Wallace with an effective right hook while yelling, "You god damned loser. This is what I get for hooking up with you! With your, 'Come on honey, it's a no-brainer. We'll make a bundle from these chumps. They'll never even see it coming.' I should've known better after six years of your useless bull shit!"

One of Jim's boys, moving faster than anyone else, helped the stick of dynamite back to her seat. The ringleader of the gang rubbed his jaw with an, "aw shucks," look on his face.

Will removed a .380 semiautomatic pistol from his desk with a pencil inserted in the end of the barrel. Holding it up for observation, he asked, "Mr. Walters or if you prefer, Hakim isn't this pistol remarkably similar to the one Mr. O'Connor took from you the other night at a Chinese restaurant in Wilkinsburg?"

Thinking that Will was using the pencil to preserve fingerprints, Walters said, "Yeah, that's the one."

Will frowned, looked at the gun, returned his gaze to Walters and said, "Now think before you answer. Your answer will have a direct influence on how and where you spend the rest of your life. Where did you get the gun?"

Morahuni, or Connie, whichever she was calling herself at the moment, made a movement as though she would answer for him, but Will hushed her with a finger to his lips.

Willie Lump-lump tried to look as though he was elsewhere while his chubby cohort merely looked sick.

Walters licked his lips, made a supplicating gesture with his hands and started to speak.

The door connecting Will's office to the waiting room was suddenly flung open and detective second grade Manfred Wolfgang Todd entered the room, gun in hand. He and said rather melodramatically, "Nobody make a move. Get your hands up."

Will answered for us all, "Which do you want, paralysis or hands in the air?"

Will continued, "Mr. Jones, Miss Fredrickson, and Mrs. Jones, permit me to introduce Detective Todd of the city police. He is working on this case. Mr. Walters, I believe you are already acquainted with him."

Walters's eyes darted around the room looking for a place to escape the wrath of Todd. He started to say, "I wasn't going to-"

"Shut up," Todd barked. He took in the entire group and said, "Thanks for your help, Barrett. I'll take it from here."

He reached under his jacket with his free hand, pulled out a pair of handcuffs, and started in Walters's direction.

Walters's eyes bulged and he said, "Don't let him take me in. He's going to kill me."

Will consoled him, "Nobody's taking anyone anywhere just yet. Relax."

"This is my prisoner and I'm taking him in," Todd barked.

Will bestowed a baleful stare upon Todd and said, "Detective Todd, look around you. Besides these four in front of my desk there are seven other people in this room. Are you so arrogant as to assume that you possess the only firearm in this room? Sit down."

Todd looked around, noticed me to his right with my hand in my jacket, Jim smiling with his right hand out of sight in the back of his waistband, and Will with his massive fist now comfortably wrapped around the .380 semiautomatic. He worked his lips a time or two, returned his pistol to its holster and sat down, but not before saying, "This is tantamount to conspiracy to resist arrest."

Will returned the pistol to a place out of sight and, just to be conversational, nodded agreement and asked, "Where's Shallenberger?"

Todd said his partner hadn't been at the office when the call came in from Will.

"Now then, where were we?" Will asked rhetorically. Not waiting for an answer, he went on, "Where are my manners? PT, would you see if any of our guests would like something in the way of libation?"

I got up and made the rounds. Jim's fellows, grouped near the newly acquired New Bedford Whaler's ship's wheel, confined themselves to drinks that were non-alcoholic and sugar-free. Jim, hanging out by the door from the outer office, already had a tumbler of chilled fruit juice clasped in his large pugilist's hands.

The ersatz followers of Mohammed, in direct violation of the tenets of the teetotaling espousals of their religion, all claimed something sweetly alcoholic. The men each held a snifter of brandy as though they had never seen one before. The ladies of the foursome had things that were both fruity and poured over ice.

Todd, supposedly on duty, had a whiskey and water in violation of city regulations. Will already had something that looked like lemonade. I settled for iced water.

Everyone had a drink of their choice.

Will took a sip, smiled benevolently, and said, "Detective Todd, just as you were arriving, Mr. Walters was getting ready to tell us where he had acquired the pistol that PT relieved him of. Do please go on, Mr. Walters."

Walters's discomfiture was evident in his fidgeting as he squirmed around in his chair to get a look at Todd, who was seated behind him to his left. He hemmed and hawed and made a couple of false starts. It was obvious that he wasn't going to say anything in the presence of Detective Todd.

Will's voice was both conciliatory and sympathetic as he looked from Walters to Todd and back.

"It seems that Mr. Walters is a bit reticent right now for whatever reasons." He looked at everyone in turn. "With the able assistance of everyone in this room, I'll try to fill in the blanks. Furthermore, those people present who have been unjustly accused of various activities may receive their just apologies. And, finally, some people present may even profit from this gathering."

At this point a high backed armchair to Will's right swiveled around to reveal an elderly black man sipping from a mint julep. His mischievous eyes were smiling brightly.

# CHAPTER 21 - WINNERS AND LOSERS

Will pushed a button on his telephone console. The door opened and the two more people entered. Every male eye in the room followed Pamula and Beth's progress to their respective positions. Pamula took up a position on a chair to Will's left. Beth settled in next to me against the wall near the Lockes.

"For those few of you who don't know him, allow me to introduce Mr. Clarence Darrow Reynolds, an old friend of my family who has been enduring pain at the hands of a number of you." Will's dissatisfaction with anyone who would cause discomfort to a friend of his was evident in the intensity of his gaze as it fleetingly rested in turn on the Keepers of the Koran, Danny Saint Martin, the Lockes and Detective Todd.

Will then said, "The purpose of this meeting is to bring that pain to an end."

Unk was having a good time and smiled at everyone in the room, raising his glass in a mock toast.

Will centered his doodling pad on his desk and frowned at it before saying, "A couple of weeks ago, Mr. Reynolds came to me and told me that someone was trying to strong arm him into selling his business interests at a deflated price…"

Will then gave a brief summary of Unk's troubles. He then turned the floor over to me. I left my spot beside Beth and walked to the front of Will's desk where I could face everybody.

Raising my glass of iced water in his direction, I said, "Mr. Saint Martin's associates, Mosticello and McClymonds were the instruments of Mr. Reynolds' original discomfort."

Danny tried to make himself inconspicuous, which was difficult seeing that he was dressed like a Southern politician of yore, including the cream double-breasted suit and wide-brimmed hat which he nervously tapped with his fingers. He flashed his artificially whitened teeth when everyone else glanced in his direction.

"But," I continued, "They were not the source of it. The source of Mr. Reynolds' discomfort was more ambiguous than that. Will has my report on that."

Will took up where I left off.

"Yes. It goes back a little farther than that. It seems that one Kyle Snyder had a job in the city's department of computer services. In fact, he was an assistant director of the department. He had access to the entire city's computer traffic, including encrypted files."

As Will glanced down at his notes I saw Mrs. Locke out of the corner of my eye wriggling her Fox Chapel by way of Morningside butt deeper into her chair. Her husband had her right hand in his left hand, showing white spots on his knuckles.

Will encompassed the entire assemblage in his story. "Mr. Snyder learned that a certain piece of property in the South Side was ideally situated for either of two large construction projects being bandied about in private communications within the mayor's office: a new sports and condominium complex or a legalized gambling center replete with housing and entertainment, Vegas style."

The four in the front row were completely at a loss trying to figure how they had anything to do with Will's summation. Will smiled at them and indicated with a raised finger that they were still on his mind. He would get back to them.

Nodding in my direction, he said, "PT figured out that Kyle took his information to the Gummert Construction Company. This heads-up gave them an unfair early warning and allowed them to be in the catbird seat when bidding for the project started.

"Mr. Snyder had a limited view of the value of his information and was content with the reward of a good job that Gummert gave him."

I guessed that Vivien Locke thought any offense was a good defense because right about here she gave a wave of dismissal and said, "I don't see what all this b.s. has to do with us."

Will placated her by raising his left hand palm outward and saying, "All in good time dear. All in good time."

He again indicated that I should take up the cudgel by nodding in my direction and saying, "PT, if you would."

I took a sip of iced water and cleared my throat. "Snyder was self-serving and small time. Being that kind of guy, he couldn't keep his mouth shut. If he had we wouldn't be here. He blabbed the whole thing to his wife Trish to show her what a great guy he was."

Now Vivien could see the direction the conversation was taking and took a large gulp from her glass of Glenlivet over ice. A bit must've gone up her nose because she gagged and snorted like a pig rooting for truffles for a few seconds. When she regained her composure, I said, "Here is where you come in, Mrs. Locke. Your sister was jealous of your success in marrying into money, so she called everyone in the family and bragged about how smart her hubby was and generally spilled the beans."

"When you heard the news, you immediately saw the possibilities within your brother-in-law's information. Where he saw a job, you saw dollars, lots of them."

She tried to stifle a smile when she heard the words, "dollars." She wasn't successful.

"So, Mrs. Locke, you passed a lot of the information you had gotten from your sister on to your husband. He, in turn, upped production of structural steel to put his company in a favorable bidding position when the construction contracts were awarded."

The not overly long attention span of the Keepers of the Koran had run out along with the contents of their glasses. Messrs. Walters and Jones were content to relieve their boredom by wistfully examining the lack of contents in their glasses. Inactivity however, wasn't Miss Frederickson's forte.

She jumped up, placed her hands on her nearly nonexistent hips, and said directly in Will's face, "What's all this crap got to do with us? I ain't putting up with this and you ain't got no reason to keep me here."

Walters put his face in his hands and muttered plaintively, "Connie, please. For once in your life would you please just shut up?"

She turned on him, having found a familiar target for her wrath. Before she could lash out, Pamula had wrapped her in a less than sisterly embrace. Pinning Connie's arms against her side, Pamula cooed into her ear, "Come on, hon, let's us girls get away from these bozos."

The two of them left the office for the front lounge. Mary Jones toddled along in their path like a duckling following its mother.

Big Jim smiled and, taking advantage of the chance to rest his dogs, settled into one of the newly vacated seats between Walters and Jones. He included them in his circle of comfort by draping his arms across the backs of their chairs.

"Women," he commented good naturedly, "Can't live with 'em, can't live without 'em, right guys?" He punctuated his sentence by knuckling both Walters and Jones on their shoulders.

Beth shifted from one foot to the other. The way she screwed up her lips showed that Jim's attempt at levity had fallen flat, at least with her.

Once again Will took control and returned order to the meeting. He said, "PT, you were saying?"

"Thanks, Will. Being loyal to her roots, and seeing a chance to pick up a chunk of cash all her own in this affair, Vivien called on an old school flame and dropped a dime in Mr. Saint Martin's direction."

Wallace Locke turned to look at the flamboyant Saint Martin much as a wren might examine a cardinal. I think it was the word, "affair," that caught his attention. It crossed my mind that, while a wren may not be the most admired of birds, neither is it a good target. Protective coloration and all that.

"Part of Danny's thanks to Vivien was seeing to it that her brothers as well as her other sister's husband were taken care of, job wise."

Vivien smiled at that, no doubt taking pride in her familial devotion.

The ball was now back in Will's court and he picked up where I left off. I circulated among the now mostly male group refreshing drinks and checking for reactions.

"Mr. Saint Martin needed capital to take proper advantage of the situation. He went looking to out-of-town sources for funding so that the cement company he owned in his mother's name could make ready for the project."

Will smiled in Danny's direction showing his understanding of the necessity of working capital.

"The out-of-towners immediately saw past Mr. Saint Martin's ambition, realizing that whoever owned the property was going to be in a position to make literally millions of dollars," Will said.

"As part of the vigorish for the loan, Mr. Saint Martin was instructed to pick up the property on the q.t. for a song."

Danny's composure was showing the first signs of weakness. Up to this point he had been happy, comfortable and relaxed. When Will mentioned the out of town money, the smile left Danny's eyes and, instead of sparkling, they glittered.

Will smiled at his discomfiture and said, "Mr. Saint Martin decided to pick it up for a real short song and went in for some old time muscle tactics."

As an aside to Danny, Will commented, "That stuff went out of style years ago. And one thing I always thought you had was style."

Danny sipped at his new martini, set the glass down on the side table, and mouthed the word, "Sorry," in Will's direction.

Will nodded assent at Danny's contrition and said, "Therein lies his major mistake. He brought undesirable pressure to bear on someone I consider family. I take it personally when my family is threatened. I decided then and there that Mr. Saint Martin would not profit from his involvement in this venture. Mr. O'Connor joined me in this endeavor."

I glanced in Issac's direction and saw that he was still with one of Jim's boys behind Todd. Todd meanwhile, was doing his utmost to seem simultaneously bored and attentive. His nervousness was evident in the way he was chewing the inside of his cheek.

It was my turn again, "Between the Kurhansky sisters, brothers, brothers-in-law, spouses, lovers, and friends, the number of people in the conspiracy had gotten unwieldy. All this activity in the construction sector had come to the attention of one of the string-pullers in the mayor's office.

"What had started out to be a cozy little money maker for a few politicos and their cronies seemed to be almost public knowledge. Everyone was in on it except the mayor himself, who was off somewhere making deals with department stores.

"Things had to be reined in. Orders were passed down the line to stifle the competition coming from Saint Martin's direction."

The Lockes were visibly more relaxed now, what with the heat being directed elsewhere. Wallace Locke, for the first time, seemed to become aware of the richness of his surroundings. Some of Will's seafaring artifacts had whetted his engineer's attention.

I raised my voice to recapture their wandering attention.

"The original plan was to knock off Mosticello and McClymonds as a warning to Saint Martin.

"A fall guy with a plausible motive was needed. Enter Lorenzo Walters or, if you will, Hakim. Word was all over the street that McClymonds had welshed on a payoff to Walters for $10,000 that Walters had won on a sucker bet with him. Somehow or other, McClymonds had screwed up the scam and, instead of pocketing $500 of Walters's money, wound up owing him ten grand."

I walked around to the front of the room and leaned against Will's desk so that Walters and Jones wouldn't have to keep swiveling around in their chairs to see me. Their fidgeting was getting on my nerves.

I continued, "So McClymonds skipped out on the bet. Walters was bellowing to anybody who'd listen how he was going to cut out McClymonds' heart and eat it while McClymonds watched."

Walters smiled in memory of his bellicosity and then frowned when he realized that he was still out ten grand.

Jones tried to look dumb, which wasn't asking much from his acting repertoire.

I was still holding forth at center stage.

"A representative of the mayor's office furnished Walters with two things. The first was an untraceable gun supposedly destroyed years before. The second was a sense of invincibility since he had been promised immunity from prosecution."

I explained how Walters had been clued in on McClymonds' habit of taking Old Second Avenue on his way back to the city proper because he really liked to wind up his car and turn it loose on the unpatrolled stretches where J&L Steel used to be. Walters was tipped off the next time McClymonds went out of town. He positioned his car out of sight by the Second Avenue underpass where Greenfield Avenue and Saline Street intersect it.

"OK, folks, now stay with me because it gets complicated here."

I took a sip from my ice water and felt Will's eyes drilling into my back admonishing me to speed it up.

I said, "Imagine Walters' confusion when he first saw McClymonds' car come barreling through the underpass. Just as he was ready to follow, I came through following through with me on McClymonds' tail. Then, when he tried to pull out for the second time a third car came hurtling through with its lights out following me.

"Walters joined the convoy to see what was going down. Here's what he saw.

"Instead of rocketing along as fast as his car would go, McClymonds kept his speed under 80 miles an hour so his henchmen could overtake me.

"Just before the long straightaway under the Birmingham Bridge, Walters saw a shotgun blast fired into my car. My car then gave a splendid impersonation of a drunken ballerina cavorting, pirouetting and just generally ricocheting off everything in sight before finally resting against a pile of gravel."

Locke's attention was wandering again while his wife was trying to get my attention with a flash of thigh sent my way like a signal beacon. I smiled my appreciation and continued to explain how Walters watched Mosticello and McClymonds drag me from the wreckage of my car and add a few more lumps and bruises to my fresh collection. I apologized to those in attendance because the rest of my account of that evening's proceedings was based on conjecture and reconstruction. I was elsewhere at the time.

"I have been told by a fairly unreliable source that Mosticello returned to his car, having no stomach for the way McClymonds was getting off on working over an unconscious man. While I personally doubt Monticello's sudden attack of decency, the facts fit it.

"Anyhow, as McClymonds was busy with me, Walters sneaked up behind him and shot him in the back of the head."

Jim gave the men in the front row a great big squeeze from his position between them and chuckled while he said, "Ain't you guys something?"

Jim always could see a bit of levity where no one else could.

I resumed, "Mosticello mistook Walters for the guys with the shotgun and thought he was next in line for some ballistic plastic surgery. He left as fast as he could and has been hiding out since."

Saint Martin gave me a thumbs-up at my interpretation of events.

"Walters then pushed me into a concrete form nearby. He thought it would be cute to put McClymonds' body in the trunk of my car.

"His total take from the murder was a couple of twenties from me and whatever he found on McClymonds, including McClymonds gun. He took out his frustration on McClymonds head with the jack handle in the trunk before closing the lid.

"Then for whatever reason, maybe because he was still suffering from a decency attack, Mosticello called this office and left a message about where I could be found."

I sighed and moved to the left of Will, having come to the end of my recitation. Others in the room sighed appreciatively as well realizing that they would no longer have to hear me expostulate.

Todd smiled expansively and made a twirling motion with his right forefinger in the air.

"What a load of crap. Now, if you will excuse me, I'll be taking the prisoner in for processing."

He made a move as to get up, but Issac sort of leaned on his shoulders, helping him to remain seated.

"Not so fast, Detective Todd," Will said. "Aren't you curious as to how PT arrived at his conclusions? Conclusions that I share, by the way."

He replied, "I couldn't care less how some two-bit PI twists facts to be able to bill a client. All I know is that you've got a shooter here and I'm taking him in."

A new arrival provided a distraction when his voice from the back of the room said, "I don't think so, partner."

Shallenberger strode across the room, relieved Issac of his position behind Todd and deftly stripped Todd of his gun and handcuffs. He then handcuffed a protesting Todd with Todd's own handcuffs.

Saint Martin, figuring that the meeting was over, made a move to leave, but was stopped in his tracks by an utterance from Will, "Don't."

Vivien decided to make her break, but ran up against an obstacle in the form of Beth who did something weird with her hands that resulted in Vivien's lying face down on the floor sobbing with frustration.

Walters couldn't even move from Jim's grasp and Jones continued to do what he did best: look dumb.

Wallace Locke already had his cell phone in his hand dialing his attorney.

Will crossed those mahogany tree trunks he calls arms and smiled benevolently as the round-up continued while Unk laughed and looked as though he hadn't had this much fun in decades.

I simply marveled at the efficiency displayed by Shallenberger, Exie and the squad of plainclothes officers, men and women, as they cleared the office of malefactors.

As things wound down, Pamula came through the door in possession of Danny Saint Martin's overly muscled chauffeur.

"I think you guys forgot something," she said as she handed him over to one of Exie's men. She pulled a wicked looking pistol equipped with a banana clip from her waistband and handed it to the officer.

"When all the law enforcement showed up and I gave them the ladies I had been entertaining, I noticed this pretty boy on one of the monitors sneaking around to the back of the building, where he had parked Saint Martin's car. I thought someone would like to talk to him, so I went and got him."

The detective took in this gorgeous example of feminine beauty and said, "You shouldn't have done that. You might have gotten hurt. Leave apprehending prisoners to the professionals."

She fixed him with a look that could wilt sunflowers and said, "Yeah, right."

After things had settled a bit, Exie came over to me and said, "Shallenberger and I watched the entire performance on the monitor at Pamula's desk. It was splendid. Now I just hope that you can prove those allegations."

In my best imitation of Big Jim Snyder, I gave him a hearty hug around his neck and said, "Ya better believe it, pilgrim."

# CHAPTER 22 - HORSES AND GATES

The case was pretty well wrapped up. By the time we were all finished with depositions, interviews, statements and whatnot, it was well into the early hours of Sunday. When I finally got home, I cleaned-up a bit and crashed onto my living room couch for nearly 18 straight hours. Then I only got up long enough to crawl into bed for another 8 hours.

Eventually Monday morning arrived and, with it, a new week. I broke my habit of early arrivals and got settled at my desk at 11AM. In less time than it takes to tell it, I was interrupted.

"PT, come on out here and take a look at the monitor."

Immediately to the left of her desk was a bank of four TV monitors, each connected to one of the surveillance cameras ringing our building.

In no particular hurry, I moseyed out to her location. As I approached her desk, she snapped in my direction, while pointing at the monitor on the upper right, "Come on, time isn't standing still just for you."

I hurried around to her side and looked over her shoulder at the screen. It filled with an overview of the little compound in the back where we park our cars.

"Watch this."

She fiddled with a couple of dials and centered my brandy-new, although non-descript looking car in the screen.

"You called me out here to admire my car?"

"Put a lid on it, PT. Look at the right rear quarter."

Because of the location of the camera, the right side of the car was hard to see, but a close look revealed the top of someone's head that was kneeling on the ground near the right rear tire.

"Damn, that thing doesn't even have 500 miles on it," I said, making for the back door that leads to the little lot.

"Wait a minute," she called, "Get back here. That's not all."

I returned and she panned the camera, showing where the intruder had somehow caused the remote controlled gate to open.

"OK Now watch this."

The camera panned over to the other side of the lot where Will had parked his car alongside a couple of the company sedans. Someone dressed in dark clothes and wearing a hoodie was creeping around the vehicles. It seemed as though that person was maneuvering to get behind the first person.

"O.K. Pamula. What's going on?"

"I don't know. What do you want to do about it?"

We called Will from his office, put our heads together and came up with a spur of the moment plan.

It seemed simple enough. We would all be in communication with portable radios, Will positioning himself at the back door leading to the parking compound. I would walk around the building to the automatic gate at the entrance to the compound.

When everyone was in position, Pamula would override the gate electronics and close it. At the same time I would run through the gate and grab the intruder to the right of the gate while Will would barge through the back door and apprehend the intruder in the vicinity of my car. It was uncomplicated and should've worked without a hitch.

The execution of the plan was less than perfect and, instead of being an exercise in simplicity was an exercise of simpletons.

I slunk my way around the building, past the front of Scotty's, across the front of the abandoned five and dime and down the alley to the back. The six foot high wooden fence gave me plenty of cover as I edged toward the open gate. I prepared to sprint through the gate and gave the word to the other two.

Will voice whispered through the radio, "Ready." Next was Pamula's voice saying only one word, "Now."

The big chain link gate began grinding and ratcheting closed. That's when things got weird. Anyhow, five minutes later found Will and I grouped at Pamula's desk while tears of merriment cascaded down her face while gasping sobs of laughter erupted from her as she tried in vain to catch her breath.

Rubbing at a scrape on the side of my face while mourning the destruction of a fifty dollar pair of pants, I complained, "It isn't all that funny."

This brought renewed paroxysms of laughter while she choked out the statement, "Oh, yes it is."

That's about the time that I noticed Will's brilliant white shirt covered with parking lot grime and the very tip of his nose rubbed raw.

Before I knew it, I had collapsed onto Will and he onto me as the two of us joined Pamula in hysterical revelry.

When we finally regained something approximating composure, we reviewed the tapes that had been the source of Pamula's hilarity.

The tape started with the camera zoomed out to include the entire parking area which is some forty by forty feet square. I was skulking in the area of the gate at the top of the screen while some movement showed the locations of the intruders in pretty much the same locations as before.

With a jerky motion, in fits, starts and stops, the gate staring closing. I ran through the opening as the gate was closing, heading in the direction of my car. Will charged into the camera's field of view at the bottom of the screen heading to the left. As I ran down the left side of my car, the intruder stood up at the right rear and I dove across the trunk trying to grab him. Now, I don't know if my foot caught on something or what, but somehow or another I wound up sliding across the trunk like I was on a waxed bowling alley. As I was trying to uncompress myself from the crumpled heap I found myself in, the intruder ran up the hood of my car onto the roof and then pulled himself over the wooden fence adjacent to it.

At the same time, Will was heading for the other intruder like a freight train on full throttle. He was so intent on the intruder that he didn't even see the carpenter's horse that was straddling a freshly patched pothole and entangled himself in it. He skidded face down across the parking lot surface while the other intruder escaped through the last few open inches of the closing gate.

By that time I had regained my feet and attempted to apprehend the person who ran through the closing gate. I dove for the gate and pulled myself up and over it. As I was descending the other side of the gate, my pants leg caught in the twisted wire at the top of the chain links.

The net result was that I wound up hanging upside down on the outside of the gate as my pants leg slowly ripped, dropping me to the ground.

Once we got everything sorted out, we found that the valve stem on the right rear tire of my car was sliced off. Other than that, the intruders had no time to do any additional mischief.

All-in-all it was an ignominious experience that we knew Pamula would never allow us to forget.

Pamula was forcing us to watch the tape for the third time and, while she was still enjoying it, Will and I were rapidly losing interest in this particular cinematic masterpiece. A glance at the monitor opposite the one holding Pamula's attention revealed some sort of commotion going on on the sidewalk in front of our offices. It looked like the beat cop had his hands full of a pair of perpetual motion machines.

Will and I both got to his aid at the same time, but Scotty from next door had beaten us and had one of the individuals wrapped up in his muscular arms. I noticed Scotty's friend, his sawed-off baseball bat, leaning against a parked car.

"What's up Carter? Need a hand?" Will inquired while the huge ex-Pitt football defensive lineman in the city police uniform dangled a squirming, spitting, kicking, swearing wildcat from his left hand.

"Thanks Will. I don't think so. This pair seems to belong to you," he replied.

Will's eyebrows shot skyward with disbelief as he asked, "How so?"

About that time, the handful that Scotty was restraining started yelling, "Mr. O'Connor. Mr. O'Connor. Tell 'em who I am. You know me. Jim sent me. I caught the one what was bustin' up your car."

I walked over and untangled his face from the hoodie sweatshirt that had gotten up over his head in the struggle.

"Let him go Scotty, I know this one. He won't go anywhere," I said. Then to Scotty's prisoner, "Carlos, what in the hell are you doing here?"

Will interjected, "Let's take this inside. No need for us to be entertainment for the neighborhood."

Three minutes later and we were all in Will's office. That is, all except for Scotty, who returned to his bartending duties with Officer William "Ice Cold" Carter's thanks.

Carlos and the other individual were in the hot seats previously occupied by the members of the fictitious religious sect known as, "The Keepers of the Koran."

"Ice, is there anything we can get for you? Something cold to drink, maybe?" I asked.

"I'm on duty, so I'd better just have a Pepsi or something. You know how the shoo-flies are – a snitch on every corner."

He took his Diet Pepsi and leaned against the door jamb, effectively blocking the entire doorway.

"PT, don't forget our guests here. See if they would like some sort of refreshment."

"Carlos, a glass of vegetable juice, right?"

He nodded, and I turned to our other guest, who had his face obscured with a watch cap that was pulled low and a turtleneck that was pulled high, only offering a pair of steely-grey eyes for the world's observation.

"And, what can I get for our mysterious friend, here?" I asked as I pulled the watch cap off his head, exposing a cascade of shoulder-length naturally platinum blonde hair.

He was a she. And, she looked to be about sixteen years old.

And she came exploding out of the chair, all feet, fangs and claws headed in my direction while screaming, "You no good son of a bitch. I'll f-----g kill you."

Will looked uncomfortable as I retreated in the face of this tornadic attack reminiscent of Warner Brother's Tasmanian Devil, complete with unintelligible snarls.

Ice merely leaned against the door jamb smiling and enjoying the performance while I yelled for Pamula's help.

Carlos, having more bravery than sense for the second time today, entered the whirlwind in an attempt to quell it.

Eventually the cavalry in the guise of Pamula rode to the rescue, subdued the little hellion and returned her to her chair.

Giving her most saccharine smile, Pamula informed her, "Honey, if you can't behave yourself, you're going to find yourself handcuffed to that chair."

Arms crossed, she slumped in the chair letting her breath out in an explosive huff.

Having regained his composure, Will pinioned her with his glare and said, getting louder as he went on, "O.K. young lady, we've just about had it up to here with your shenanigans. Who are you and what in the hell is going on?"

He emphasized his question by smacking the palms of his hands on his desk threateningly.

I had to hand it to her. She didn't even flinch. She just stuck her lower lip out a bit more and, looking him straight in the eyes, muttered, "I don't have to tell you anything."

Ice, sensing that he had the hole card, strode around to the front of Will's desk and, leaning back against it with his arms folded, smiled at her and said, "Maybe not, sweetie. However, you have to tell me. I can tell from the way you're dressed that you don't want to sit in the detention center overnight with all the teenie bopper hookers, junkies and gang-bangers that wind up there.

"You see, I can tell that you're from the 'burbs and those city kids wouldn't take kindly to you. Although they might like your sneakers and designer jeans."

Then, in a reasonable tone, he asked, "So, why don't you just come clean with us? We'll call your daddy and he can meet us at the zone office and take you home, OK?"

Tears streaming through the smudges of dirt on her face, she regained her feet, spun around pointing at me and spat, "Because that bastard put my daddy in jail. That's why."

Oh boy. Just what I was missing from my life. A pissed-off hysterical teenager looking for revenge.

Exasperatedly I asked, "Just who in the hell are you?"

"I'm Jack Blackburn's daughter, but I guess that doesn't mean anything to you," she spat back.

In a flash the whole thing came back to me: chop shops, insurance fraud, the fraud squad, happy insurance executives and jail time for Jack Blackburn.

"Yeah, it means something to me," I muttered, but didn't elaborate.

It took a bit of doing, but we got things sorted out. I called Beth and told her that a minor was going to need her help, legal and otherwise. I filled her in as best as I was able and told her that the Ice Man was going to take the juvenile to Zone Six before transporting her to Juvenile Detention. Beth said that she'd do what she could.

Another phone call to Jim Shepherd and Carlos' situation was all squared away and he got a ride back to the Bottoms with my thanks. Before he left, he showed us where the teenaged tornado had parked her little urban scooter. She'd stashed it behind the building across the street in a little cubicle that at one time had held a couple of garbage cans.

Now this thing was a real piece of work. About the size of a kid's sidewalk scooter, it had a headlamp, a brake light, turn signals and a little pedestal seat. It was equipped with a little two-stroke chainsaw type engine and had a gas tank that held about a quart. It was the ideal vehicle for dashing around a crowded city, zipping in and out of traffic and ignoring back-ups.

It cleared up a lot of things that had been buzzing around in my head. Like that pesky mosquito whine I heard every time some little thing or another in my life would cause me aggravation.

# CHAPTER 23 - BRIGHT IDEAS (MAYBE NOT SO)

Figuring that everything was being taken care of, and leaving the details to Beth, Will and Pamula, I blissfully put the entire affair out of my mind.

Bright and early on a Monday morning a week later and I was cheerfully behind my desk once again ready to face whatever came my way.

Life was good and all my batteries were recharged. It was Gauley Season and the Summerville Dam had been drawing down in anticipation of the winter snow pack and the resulting spring melt. Friday and Saturday found me and groups of likewise mis-minded folk gleefully cavorting in the 3,000 cubic foot per second of water released into that world class whitewater river.

Though I had garnered a few scrapes and bruises in the effort, body, mind and soul was now ready to face anything in my current karmic condition.

I had even stopped on the way in and bought a dozen freshly-baked bagels at a New York style deli on the way in, my treat.

I checked the weekend's electronic avalanche of email and cleared my in box of as much spam as possible with a cursory examination, then winnowed it farther by deleting all the commercial appeals to my wallet. It took me nearly fifteen minutes of my extremely valuable time, but I finally reduced six hundred and some emails to eighteen worth reading. I then tackled the accumulation of snail mail. That only took five minutes. Then my stack of telephone messages. Two and a half hours of solitary desk work later and my karma was staring to tarnish. I was entertaining thoughts of bad juju, but couldn't figure how to make a voodoo doll that represented paperwork.

My intercom blinked. It was Will.

"P.T., stop in here when you get a minute, OK?"

That meant now, so I replied, "On the way, boss."

I renewed my mug of coffee, blew by Pamula's deserted desk, glommed a bagel and went in to Will's office.

He sat beatifically behind his desk with Pamula standing with her left hand lightly resting on his right shoulder. Except for the smug expression on their faces and the twinkle in Pamula's eyes, it could almost pass for the posing of a formal portrait. Something was up.

That usually meant unwanted additional work for me.

"Sit down, PT. Pamula and I have been putting our heads together and we have decided that your work load is getting a bit, shall we say, unwieldy."

Uh-Oh. I kept my reaction to myself and merely grunted around a mouthful of bagel that I agreed.

"To this end, we have decided that it is beyond Pamula's ability to stem the tide and that you need an office assistant of your own."

It's hard to smile around a mouthful of bagel, so I washed it down with a swallow of coffee and indicated my pleasure with an ear to ear smile. I wasn't speechless. It's just that my mind was racing so far ahead of them that I couldn't, for the minute, talk. I was already trying to decide whether I wanted someone elegantly and beautifully competent like Della Street or an obvious sexual distraction like Richard Diamond's receptionist. I was mentally cataloging body types, hair color and styles and deciding whether warm brown eyes or sexy green eyes would better adorn my office.

Will was still talking.

"So we have gotten you an office assistant that will be able to handle most of your paperwork, take your calls and arrange your schedule."

He pushed a button on his desk that caused a faint buzzing in the outer office and said, "PT, meet your new executive office assistant."

The door to his office opened inward and Beth strode in exhibiting everything that my wildest dreams could conjure in the way of an office assistant. Then it immediately flashed across my mind: would I want a so-called helper that was smarter than I?

Beth turned back to the door and said, "Come on honey, he won't bite."

Then, demurely stepping across the threshold was a five foot four, one hundred and fifteen pound, platinum blonde picture of youthful innocence.

The last time I had seen this vision of lamblike guilelessness, Pamula and Carlos were peeling her off me in order to save my rugged good looks from the life and limb shredder she had become.

I looked aghast from Will to Pamula to Beth and back to Will, saying, "Wait just one little minute here. You want me to sit in the same space as that little hellion who'll just be waiting for me turn my back to offer a target for her knife?"

Blondie spoke up for herself and said, "I told you the no good son of a bitch wouldn't go for it."

Beth countered, "Watch your language Sweetie. Remember what we agreed on?" Then to me, "Would you just shut up and listen for a change? You just might like what you hear."

I doubted it, but I shut up just to protect what was left of my love life.

Pamula, continuing to beam like a sun eliminating darkness, said, "PT, I don't think you two have been properly introduced."

She walked to the doorway and, arm around her shoulders, escorted the silver-topped fiend to the front of will desk and said, "Allow me to present your new office assistant and secretary, Miss Philomena Blackburn."

The girl held her hand out to shake mine smiling and saying, "If you ever call me anything but Phill, I'll kill you."

# CHAPTER 24 - BEST LAID PLANS

A few weeks went by. I was as nervous as a one-legged man at an ass kicking contest and as busy as a hooker at a political convention.

I straightened out the problem with the insurance company with a bit of creative bookkeeping and an envelope with a stamp canceled before the bill was due. Removing the previous return and addressee labels was no problem. Likewise affixing the firm's return address and a new address label for the insurance company was a piece of cake.

The only thing left to do was arrange for the envelope to turn up in the insurance company's mail room. People sometimes forget that everyone can help them at some time or another. They spend all their time being nice to CEOs, VPs, and managers while they forget who really runs organizations. It's the grunts in the trenches. The file clerks, mail room clerks, phone operators, secretaries, customer service reps and sales staff who keep a corporation running. A bottle, a bouquet or a box of candy can go a long way when it winds up in the hands of someone usually overlooked in the grand scheme of things. Suffice it to say that the envelope turned up just where I wanted it.

Once that happened, the policy cancellation was rescinded with apologies all around (which I graciously accepted on behalf of the firm).

I had a few minutes to myself, so I was reading one of my whitewater guidebooks, looking for a stream that might be running during this, the driest time of year. With the weather we had been having lately I was going to be pretty much limited to streams controlled by dam releases. It was too early for the annual draw-down at dams in preparation for the winter snows, so it looked like I was headed to the Lower Youghiogheny, along with every other whitewater enthusiast for hundreds of miles. Oh well, the Lower Yough has a special place in my heart, having been the first real whitewater that I paddled.

Pamula buzzed me. I picked up the phone and heard, "PT, come on out to the front. You've got to see this."

When I got there, she merely handed me a copy of the morning's Trib folded to an inside page. I perched sideways on the corner of her desk to read it.

The article mentioned that one Regis J. McKinley Reading Society was in violation of numerous city, county and commonwealth codes relative to running an eating and drinking establishment. There was also a fuss about a fraudulent issuance of an occupancy permit. Furthermore, the city fire inspectors had found quite a number of serious violations of the fire code on, in, and around the premises. Various building inspectors representing plumbing, heating, electrical and structural disciplines located violations ranging from electrical service boxes not mounted perfectly level to drain pipes not meeting the specified drop per foot. And so on.

The net result, according to one certain smug so-called investigative reporter, was that the club would be losing its occupancy and health permits as well as its restaurant and liquor licenses. The building itself would probably be condemned.

I made a mental note to see to it that one particular world-weary waitress cum gate keeper trying to make a living at the fake diner on the first floor of the club got a job offer. No reason for her to suffer from Danny's transgression.

The flecks in Pamula's eyes twinkled like gold dust in a prospector's pan as she mentioned, "You wouldn't call that overkill, would you?"

I chuckled all the way back to my desk where my weekend getaway was waiting for me. I picked-up the guidebook once again and thought about running the river. I would start with a launch off the high rock directly across from the put-in, then play my way through the fast running riffles of Entrance Rapids. Then the drops and holes of Cucumber Rapids. If I went by the system of an old paddling buddy name of Jeff and played at every riffle, wave, drop, eddy, and hole along the way, this first three-quarters of a mile of river would eat up a couple hours of my time. Then-

Then the phone chirped.

"Hello, Mr. O'Connor's office. Miss Blackburn speaking. How may I direct your call?"

I had to hand it to her. Her telephone manner was impeccable.

She called across the office, "It's for you, asshole."

I picked up the phone and said, "O'Connor here."

"Good day, Mr. O'Connor. You are moving up in the world. What with a secretary and all." It was Exie.

"What's up, guy." I hoped this wasn't going to take long. I was getting into my outdoorsy mode.

"First off, I want to thank you for letting me in on this case. It'll be a real feather in my cap."

I mumbled something appropriately humble, thanking him for all his assistance, all the while looking longingly at the pictures of whitewater in the Yough Gorge.

Exie said, "Lorenzo Walters and his sidekick, William Jones, finally got their wish."

I wished I could get my wish of paddling my Cruise Control Kayak through the 55 degree water some 50-odd miles from my office.

He went on, "Yep. They are no longer small time hoods. They are now squarely in the major leagues with everything but the kitchen sink being thrown at them: robbery, theft, criminal conspiracy, receiving stolen property, violations of the uniform firearms act and a bunch of lesser included offenses."

Might as well let him go on to the end, he was on a roll. I sighed, cradled the phone in the crook of my neck and looked longingly across my office to the wall where I keep my collection of broken kayak paddles.

I grunted something encouraging. At least I hoped it sounded encouraging.

"Huh? Whatever. As soon as we were done talking with them, the boys from the ATF, FBI and Homeland Security wanted to interview them concerning a plot to overthrow the United States Government by means of force, alliance with a known terrorist organization and complicity in the hijacking of an interstate shipment of firearms."

I mentioned how those boys were going to spend a bit of time where freedom doesn't reign. I was starting to feel that I would be spending quite a chunk of time in this office before I saw the light of day. I commiserated with them. Not really.

"All their involvement was corroborated by a certain material witness who is now considered to have been an unwitting and harmless co-conspirator who was duped into believing that their aims were racial harmony, religious tolerance and equal rights."

My wandering attention focused on his last statement. I interrupted him, "Wait a minute. You let that mealy-mouthed, cowardly bag of bones walk?"

He placated, "We had to make a deal with someone on the inside. You know how these things work. It was the only way we could do it and honor Will's request to keep the Howard girl out of it."

Damn. I pushed the guidebook away from me and hoped that he

wouldn't finish by dredging up some pithy little aphorism of his mother and mine.

"You know what Mom used to say, PT: sometimes it takes a thief to catch a thief."

With that I said goodbye and reached for my guidebook once again. I started going over the things I would need: boat (naturally), paddle, dry skirt, PFD (life jacket), paddling jacket and helmet-

The intercom buzzed. Phill intercepted the message and forwarded her version of it to me.

"Some city pig wants to see you."

I sighed once again, shoved my checklist away, and said, "Show him in."

Shallenberger entered, crossed my office and stuck out a big beefy hand in greeting. "Hi, O'Connor. Just thought I'd drop by and give you an update."

I shook his hand, more convinced than ever that his name should've been Brannigan. He just looked as Irish as Paddy's pig.

"You know, without your assistance, even with my undercover assignment, we might have never been able to root out the corruption in the mayor's office."

He helped himself to a cup of coffee.

"This is the best damn coffee I've ever had," he said,

"Funny how I couldn't get Todd to open up for over a year and you blew him out of the saddle in less than a month."

"It was just circumstances," I replied, "Do you want me to give you a pound?"

"I'd like that," he came back. "Would you believe that his honor the mayor didn't have a clue?"

"I'm not surprised; he never seemed to be the greedy type. I mean, after all, look where he lives."

Even though it was Wednesday, my weekend was getting farther and farther away. I slid the guidebook off the desk and returned it to its space in the book shelf to the right of my desk.

I asked, "What happened with Todd?"

Shallenberger replied, "Oh, he split wide open once we made a deal with him."

"Oh, Christ- not another deal. Isn't anyone in this case going to pay for what they actually did? What was the deal this time?"

Shallenberger hooked his forefinger between his shirt collar and neck and tugged. He almost succeeded in putting a contrite expression on his face.

"Come on, O'Connor. We do our best. We had to have some inside testimony to crack that group. Besides, the only deal we made was to promise him that he wouldn't be prosecuted as an accessory to the murder of McClymonds for furnishing Walters the gun."

He drank a bit more from his coffee and smacked his lips.

Somewhat mollified, I said, "Well, what are the charges going to be?"

"Right now it looks like a regular menu of RICO Act charges: criminal conspiracy to do at least dozen illegal things, official oppression, money laundering, tampering with evidence, and so on and so on."

Puzzled, I asked, "RICO Act?"

He replied, "Racketeering in Corrupt Organizations. It was written to end organized crime."

"End organized crime," he laughed at his own joke and went on. "It allows confiscation of any profit derived from the illegal activity. You know: cars, businesses, homes, and etcetera. Hell, I think that might even be one of the charges on Walters and Jones."

"How far up did the conspiracy go?"

His happy slurping finally got to me, Even though I didn't really want one, I went motioned to Phill to get me a cup of coffee. She gave me a one-fingered salute and went back to whatever had been occupying her time on the computer screen. So I went and got one for myself. She smiled her approval over the top of the screen.

Shallenberger swiveled around in his chair following my progress, and said, "Not to the top, if that's what you're thinking. The head honcho who dreamed up the whole thing was one Derek Crane, a deputy mayor. He's the one who came up with the idea of the independents years ago. Originally they were used to squash anyone who looked to be a future political threat to the sitting mayor."

He swiveled back in the opposite direction, following me as I returned to my desk.

"When he saw how well that was working, Crane got intoxicated with power and branched-out. This deal was his retirement plan. Swan song, so to speak."

I couldn't help myself. I interrupted, "How did his honor the mayor figure in all this?"

"He wasn't even in the loop. He thought his popularity was getting him reelected all these years while he sent the city down the old porcelain convenience."

I carefully placed my mug on an old mouse pad I use to prevent coffee rings on my desk. It's not that I'm a neat freak, it's that the desk is expensive.

Shallenberger went on to tell me all about how Todd and Crane were ratting on everybody they could think of in hope of making some more deals. Even though a fair amount of power was wielded from the office, there were only about a dozen people in on it altogether. He did say that the mayor was taking credit for rooting out the evil from the city-county building.

As Shallenberger was taking his leave, something occurred to me.

"Is your mother by any chance Irish?"

"Yeah, why?"

"No reason, just wondering."

"See ya around."

I knew it. I'll bet her maiden name was Brannigan.

I retrieved my guidebook and went back to planning my weekend.

My door opened and Will entered holding a cup of his favorite hot beverage.

"PT, got a minute?"

I sighed, returned the book to its shelf, took a sip of my not quite hot enough coffee and gave up.

"Sure 'nough, boss. What's up?"

"I just thought I'd bring you up to speed with what's happening with Uncle Clarence."

Looked like this was the day for it. I resigned myself to the fact that I was going to get nothing done in the way of personal planning and directed all my attention toward Will.

He made himself comfortable in one of my chairs, placed his cup on the side table and started.

Twenty minutes later he left and I was full of all the happily ever after information I was capable of assimilating.

One bit of unfinished business remained. I settled myself once again behind my desk, composed myself and took a couple of deep breaths before saying, "Phill, would you please come over here a minute."

She reluctantly tore herself from the computer screen, got up and trudged to my desk, standing like a penitent before me with her hands clasped behind her back.

"Phill," I said, "I know you don't want to be here. And, you know that I don't want you here. But the terms of your probation puts you here."

She made a move as to say something, but I cut her off, continuing, "So, as long as we are stuck here together, let's agree to a temporary truce, OK?"

Her eyes brimming with tears, she mumbled something derogatory about my ancestors' reproductive practices and took refuge once again behind the computer screen at her desk.

I grabbed my guide book and escaped to Scotty's for some health food: a hot sausage sandwich, fries, and cole slaw, washed down with iced tea.

It was my lucky day. There was an abandoned copy of the day's Trib on my favorite table, so I decided to catch-up on the news.

There was bad news for the local construction industry. It looked like Gummert Construction Company was going belly-up. Its stock was no longer available for OTC trading, even locally. It had something to do with overextending itself to creditors for capital purchases without corresponding income on the horizon.

The Who's News column in the business section had an announcement about a certain Jeremy MacFeinster being appointed to the position of vice president of distribution for Universal Steel. He had extensive experience in the European Division of the company in the area of scheduling and market forecasting. He would be occupying the position formerly held by Wallace Locke who would be leaving the company to pursue other objectives and to spend more time with his family.

I wiped away a bit of slaw dressing that had dribbled down my chin, nodded to the little old blue hairs who were sipping their Madeira and turned to the legal notices.

Surprise of surprises. Vivien Locke had filed for divorce from Wallace Locke. A shame, really. They were such a couple.

Enough learning for one day. I turned to the front section to find out what had happened in the city overnight.

I chomped at the hot sausage sandwich, which was overstuffed with green and red peppers and onions and managed to get a fennel seed stuck between my front teeth. As I worried it loose with my tongue, a bit of juice from the sandwich dribbled off my chin and onto the newspaper.

That drew my attention to an article that said R. R. Smith Aggregate was forced into reorganization due to not having persons with substantial financial interest in the company being listed on the company's books. A few other reasons made the list, but that was the main one. Luckily, a group of shareholders headed by Mr. Issac Bradley, a local entertainer, agreed to take over the company for an undisclosed amount of money. This would save nearly two hundred jobs on the verge of being lost to the local economy.

Enough is enough, as my dear sainted mother used to say. I wiped my chin once again, pushed the newspaper out of the way, washed away some of the spicy flavor of the sandwich with iced tea, and opened my guidebook to the appropriate page.

A tingling sensation just by my right kidney caused me discomfort. It took me a couple of seconds to realize that it was the vibration from my newly acquired cell phone. The caller ID on the phone was the office.

I slammed my book shut, picked it up, and strode for the door, yelling to anyone who would listen, "I hate cell phones!"

The patrons and staff of Scotty's Place paused to observe the source of the outburst and then returned to their diversions.

# CHAPTER 25 - FULL LIVES TO MATCH FULL BELLIES

Tempus fugit (Temp-uss few-jit, not what you're thinking). Time flies. Summer had made its last gasp and autumn had come on the scene in all its flamboyant glory before the grey of early winter. Sort of like the chrysanthemum explosion of a sky rocket before it turns to cinders.

It was the third week of October and we were all invited to a semi-formal, catered affair at Celeste's home on a chilly Thursday evening.

Will and Pamula had already arrived by the time Beth and I had deposited our coats in the foyer and joined them in the study for cocktails.

Unk sat at the large overstuffed leather chair by the ox-roast sized fireplace. He rose to give Beth a hug and a kiss and gripped my hand in a warm, firm grasp. He was literally bursting with benevolence and his smile lit the room like a beacon from a lighthouse.

"I'm so glad that the both of you could come. It is so good to see you once again," He said.

My attempt at being both humble and appropriate in my reply was interrupted when the two of us were swept up by the energetic tornado that was Celeste.

It was impossible not to smile at the torrent of bodacious goodwill that she poured upon us.

"PT, Beth it is so good to see you," she effused, "It seems like ages since the last time although it has only been three months so much has happened the last time you were here we were swimming and now winter is just around the corner."

While she paused for a breath, we each placed our drinks out of harm's way in preparation for the group hug that was imminent. I marveled at how a woman her size could completely envelope two full grown adults in her embrace. I guess a person's reach can grow to match the size of their love.

She continued, "It is so great to have everyone gathered together once again, don't you agree? The girls are here they're upstairs dressing." She took a breath, "Issac will be here soon I hope and Jeanetta's got a new young man who's been squiring her around and dinner will be soon so just make yourselves at home."

With that, she bustled away no doubt to make sure that everything was going according to plan. Beth and I both took in a much needed gulp of air, reached for our drinks and laughed when each saw what the other was doing.

A short while later a large muscular black man looking uncomfortable in a suit and tie arrived. He was escorting a medium sized caramel colored woman looking equally uncomfortable in her brightly colored, middle length dress. They both were of that hard working middle class that is more at ease in the casual atmosphere found at pool parties, bar-b-cues, communions, and baptisms than they are in what they think as drawing room society.

In no time at all Unk, Celeste, and company would see to it that they knew they were in a group of plain old people who just happened to have more money to have fun with.

"Mr. Wilson," I said, "It's great to see you again. We didn't have much of a chance to talk at our last meeting."

He ruefully rubbed at a spot on his forehead that might still be tender and shook my hand, thanking me for what he considered my life saving effort on his behalf.

He introduced his wife, saying, "Mr. O'Connor, I'd like you to meet my wife, Lilah. Honey, this is…"

She brushed past him and pinned my arms to my sides in a tearful embrace. Dabbing at her eyes as she self-consciously backed away, she said, "Ty, you don't have to tell me who this is. You've spoke about him enough in the last few weeks. Mr. O'Connor, you save my husband's life. There is nothing I can say that would ever convey my gratitude."

I could see Beth's amusement in the way her eyes crinkled at the corners as I felt myself redden with embarrassment under the onslaught. There was pride in her countenance, too.

Lilah Wilson continued, "Just remember, as long as we live, our home is your home and our family is your family."

Out of the corner of my eye I saw the EF-5 Tornado that was Celeste bearing down on our little group and, sure enough, she rescued me from the situation. In no time she had the Wilsons feeling as though they were life-long friends of hers.

I self-consciously pulled myself away from the group, attended to my drink and joined Unk in one of the chairs by the fire.

Unk raised his glass in my direction and said, "Don't be embarrassed, young man. A lot of people owe you a lot of thanks."

I mumbled something in reply, sank deeper into the cushioned leather and fixed my attention on the painting over the fireplace.

Over the next half hour, the group in the room expanded beyond those already in attendance to include Exie and his wife Maria, an Hispanic firebrand who perfectly complemented and kept his boyish enthusiasm under control.

Detective Shallenberger arrived with his wife Sharon who was his equal in every way, including size. Since the completion of the case, Beth and I had grown to know Shallenberger and his wife. I now called him, "Val," instead of, "Sir."

I was surprised to see Big Jim Shepherd in attendance and even more so when I saw the striking blonde hanging both to his arm and on every word he said. Something about the way they looked at one another convinced me that she was not a blood relative of his.

Jacquie and Jeanetta greeted Issac Bradley and another tall, slender young man who seemed familiar. That this good looking guy was the property of Jeanetta apparent from the way she possessively wrapped her arm around his bicep while introducing him as Ray to all.

The room was a repository of bonhomie, good will, mirth and people just generally comfortable in one another's company.

This mood carried over to the dinner, held in the cavernous dining room dominated by a gargantuan hand-carved walnut banquet table surrounded by a couple of dozen equally impressive chairs. Place settings for eighteen had Unk sitting at the head of the table in something more closely resembling a hand-carved throne than a dining chair.

The service was tastefully elegant, being comprised of bone china with a golden rim featuring an unobtrusive letter, "H," in gold script near the edge. This motif carried over to the crystal ware. The flatware was of muted gold plate featuring the initial, "H," only in this case it was part of the casting itself.

The steak was sumptuous, the lobster delectable, accompanied by the most perfect of wines and served with precision and discrimination by a culinary staff that exceeded all superlative description.

The most memorable part of the dinner came when Chef Karl of

Newport, Rhode Island fame wheeled out his personally-prepared dessert of custard, ice cream, and a medley of toppings, garnishments and syrups. The lights dimmed and he lit the confection producing a stupendous conflagration that sent shadows dancing along all the walls and showed flames reflected in the windows.

When the fire died out and the lights were brought back up, Chef Karl himself dished out dessert to a standing ovation.

Eventually, dinner came to a close. The table was cleared. Postprandial cocktails helped clear our palates and everyone slumped back in the chairs with comfort and contentment. None present had ever attended a more perfect dinner.

Unk, summoning our attention with a few gentle taps on the side of his crystal goblet with a spoon, interrupted the tranquil hum of conversation. All eyes turned in his direction.

"Ladies and gentlemen, first I must thank you for accepting my humble invitation to share a meal with myself and my family."

A chorus of disclaimers indicating that, indeed, the thanks were ours, was quickly waved away and he continued,

"It has been an eventful year and each of you is familiar with some of these events.

"However, other than Mr. Barrett and myself, nobody is aware of all the events that have taken place. Moreover, I have no intention of disclosing all at this gathering. The purpose of this little get together is that I may acknowledge my gratitude to you for your help with what were most assuredly very difficult times."

Embarrassment suffused the room full of people not used to getting recognition beyond the occasional pat on the back for a job well done. Some of us toyed with our cocktails while others made self conscious adjustments to their clothing.

Unk went on to say, "Most of you present have no idea what I've been up to recently.

"I have sold all my holdings on the South Side of Pittsburgh to a newly formed development corporation for a considerable sum of money. More money, in fact, than I think I will ever be able to spend."

This announcement was met with a round of applause and more than one, "Hear, hear," that was definitely tinged with apprehension from that part of the table seating the Wilsons.

Will, Pamula, Beth and I raised our glasses in his direction by way of a toast.

Unk still had the floor. The stage was his tonight.

"I have been told that the property is going to be used for a new community having condos, shopping, a marina, and featuring as a centerpiece, a new multi-use entertainment venue for concerts and other events. Oh, and did I mention that it will all be supported by a full-service casino?"

Lilah Wilson grasped her husband's hand in a white knuckled grip as she realized that the South Side Wrecking Company and Scrap Yard would be no more.

"Being a cantankerous old man and knowing that my property is greatly coveted by the developer, I made a few stipulations contingent to the sale."

It finally dawned on me where I had seen Jeanetta's new beau before. I should've made the connection earlier during introductions. His name wasn't Ray. It was Rey. Short for Reynaldo. Reynaldo Hayes, Jim Shepherd's chief trainer. I didn't recognize him in formal attire. The only thing I'd ever seen him in was workout clothes, heavy gloves and protective head gear. I gave a smile of recognition in his direction which he returned with knowing amusement.

I returned my attention to Unk.

"Will Barrett. You, Pamula and PT have saved my life, my family and my business in ways that only we are privy to. I know that my heartfelt thanks are all the remuneration that you feel is due. But, I would be remiss if I didn't at least attempt to repay you in a more tangible manner.

"Therefore, W.E.B. Enterprises will be in charge of all job site security during the construction stages of the building project. When the complex is fully operational, W.E.B. will have the responsibility for all on-site security. It is up to you, Will, to negotiate satisfactory terms for your contract."

Will beamed, Pamula patted his hand and I was speechless as Beth gave me a quick little kiss on the cheek.

Unk was far from done.

"Issac, do you have any idea how much concrete will be required for this endeavor? Enough said.

"Detectives Shallenberger and O'Reilly, you both have become trusted allies and friends. I know that your positions with the city preclude you from accepting any material thanks, at this time. But be aware that a lucrative position commensurate with your experience and qualifications within the complex awaits the conclusion of your tenure with the police force."

Val and Exie basked in the glow of pride emanating from their wives, Sharon and Marie.

Unk looked farther down the table at Jim Shepherd and said, "Mr. Shepherd, for someone such as yourself who would go to such lengths to help a friend of a friend of a friend indicates a capacity for loyalty and compassion unheard of in these times.

"I want you to know that, from this day forth, Jim's Gym will not want for anything."

With that, Jim got to his feet, and headed in Unk's direction, arms outstretched, He only took a short detour by Rey to deliver a high five en-route to delivering a bone crushing hug that lifted Unk out of his chair.

Unk eventually was able to disentangle himself from Jim's exuberant gratitude and regain his seat at the head of the table. Jim returned to his seat next to his bit of eye candy that was all over him with happiness at his good fortune.

Unk reclaimed order with a few more taps on his goblet.

"Finally, last, but by no means least, Tyler old friend, I haven't forgotten that you were ruthlessly attacked and hospitalized simply because you were one of my employees. During the construction phase and later after the project is completed, a number of persons will be needed who have experience supervising workers. You will have one of those positions. All of my former employees are guaranteed positions at least equal to those held with my company.

"Beyond this, let me again express my deepest heartfelt thanks to all of you."

Anything else he may have been tempted to add was drowned out by a standing ovation, accompanied by numerous toasts.

A telephone was stridently making its presence known in an adjacent room. Out of deference to the occasion, those of us so equipped had turned our cell phones off.

Celeste went to answer it and returned saying, "Will, it's for you."

Will returned seconds later and said, "PT, we've got to go. One of our clients, Strassmann's Jewelers over in Shadyside, has been robbed. A maintenance worker has been found dead in the adjacent apartment building, the building itself has been torched and our watchman is missing in the rubble and feared dead."

Crackle and static emanated from the just turned on Walkie Talkies of Shallenberger and O'Reilly as they and Will, Pamula, Beth and I rushed for the door sending both apologies and thanks to Uncle Clarence and his daughter Celeste.

It looked like Marie and Sharon were going to have to car pool their own way home.

The last sight that stayed with me was the expression of longing on Jim's face to join the chase.

THE END.

Watch for further adventures with P. T. O'Connor in the forthcoming novel,
"The Polish Prince."

# ABOUT THE AUTHOR

Ed Kelemen is a writer, columnist, and playwright who lives in a small West Central Pennsylvania town with his wife, two of five sons, a trio of humongous dogs and a clutch of attitude-ridden cats. His articles and short stories have appeared in numerous local, regional, and national publications. Visitors are always welcome at his website, www.ekelemen.com and he is also easily found on Facebook.